GORDON R CLARKE is, in his spare time, an international authority on banking technology and financial policy. However, he prefers to write stories and poems, play the guitar and perform in comedy revues. He has an MA in Natural Sciences from Cambridge University and a PhD in Applied Physics from City University in London. He spent his early career in information technology at the Bank of England, whence he moved to international management consulting, working for twenty years for top international firms. In the 1990s, he became a partner in Coopers & Lybrand and then PricewaterhouseCoopers in Australia. He now runs his own consulting firm based in Singapore, with occasional visits – pandemics permitting – to the 'old country'.

Born and brought up in south-east London, Gordon has lived and worked on five continents, which creates the backdrop for his writing. He now spends his time mainly in Thailand and Greece, or on-site with clients. During his career, he has published three technical books, many articles on behavioural economics, payment technology and cryptocurrencies and a number of philosophical papers on science and religion. Technology and travel inspired his early writing and, over the years, he has frequently explored his experiences in short stories and poetry. As a research student, he won a London Colleges short story competition, judged by the late Philip Larkin.

Having taken the plunge to collate his first book of short stories, Gordon is looking forward to publishing other works that have been in development over the past thirty years or more, and to making the most of his wide range of interests from financial markets and science to music and creative writing.

To follow Gordon's bl   k, please see www.manandcyb

SOMEONE ELSE'S GODS

Gordon R Clarke

To William

Good wishes from

Gordon

SilverWood

Published in 2022 by SilverWood Books

SilverWood Books Ltd
14 Small Street, Bristol, BS1 1DE, United Kingdom
www.silverwoodbooks.co.uk

ISBN 978-1-80042-145-5 (paperback)
ISBN 978-1-80042-146-2 (ebook)

British Library Cataloguing in Publication Data
A CIP catalogue record for this book is
available from the British Library

Page design and typesetting by SilverWood Books

To Cecil R Nobby *Clarke and Jean M Clarke, my parents;*
good people, whose stories are forever lost in the past.

Contents

Foreword

Over the many years I have known him – for we were at school and university together – Gordon Clarke has penned an impressive number of words, even if you exclude the many reports, papers and articles he has compiled as part of his day job in the world of banking technology. He has written, and continues to write, song lyrics (he is a talented singer/songwriter guitarist), poetry, a PhD thesis on neurotransmitters in the central nervous system, comedy sketches which he also performs, articles on diverse topics including philosophy, consciousness theory, evolutionary theory, sociobiology, theology, the science and religion debate, and politics, as well as short stories. I am delighted that it is this last category which is now being made available in *Someone Else's Gods*, for his many other interests, knowledge and abilities both underpin and permeate many of the stories contained in this volume.

A great strength of this collection is the variety of its styles and genres: from the simple twist (or twists) in the tale, to travelogue reflection, to the analysis of relationships, to one of his comedy sketches (slightly adapted from when we first performed it together), to an exploration of artificial intelligence, to science fiction. I particularly like '*The Document of Zaxtana*: An Analytical Translation', a subtle critique of today's society in an account of anthropologists reconstructing the ethos and beliefs of an earlier fictional (or is it?) civilisation. In a very different vein, he neatly rips to shreds the ubiquitous Christmas letter in the beautifully over-the-top parody 'It Can't Be Christmas Already?' The contrast of styles between these two stories is remarkable.

When I read earlier versions of several of these stories, I encouraged my polymath friend to polish them and publish them. I can at least take some credit for the fact that he has finally done so, and I unhesitatingly commend to you *Someone Else's Gods*.

RNF Skinner, author of the novel *Still Crazy...*
and (as Richard Skinner) poet and performer.

Preface

I have enjoyed short stories ever since I read a collection called *Twentieth-Century Short Stories* for GCE O Level English Literature. Being a science student, that book opened up a new world for me. Characters vividly painted in a few lines, poignant scenes sketched on a page, the tone of the voices. These were paintings with words – few, but enough to set off the imagination with the clarity of a feature film and sometimes a surprise at the end that brought a smile of satisfaction. I can still call to mind many of the images conjured by those writers – Graham Greene, EM Forster, Katherine Mansfield.

As I started to travel, I discovered Somerset Maugham's Malaysian stories, and the stories of Jorge Luis Borges and Ernest Hemingway. I also enjoyed Isaac Asimov's science fiction pieces, the quirky essays of David Sedaris, travel stories from the likes of Paul Theroux, and Victoria Hislop's evocations of Greece, one of the countries in which I feel most at home.

I have been truly fortunate to have worked in fifty countries and lived in eight during my long career. This has given me an unusual perspective on life and business across the world. Trying to help a wide range of clients to resolve difficult problems, both technical and personal, has taught me more than my fair share about the human condition. Spending time with the poor and the rich, the privileged and the forgotten, across countries with widely differing cultures, climates and levels of wealth has been enriching. Amidst those late-night struggles to find a workable answer to the impossible question, I collected the fragments of stories – stories of reality and morality, men and women, place and time.

Honing one's writing skills in the crucible of international commerce is not a bad apprenticeship for a writer – having to persuade, to make points subtly but powerfully, to be memorable – these demand wordcraft. If I had realised when I was a research student and won a London Colleges short story competition that I had some small talent as a writer, perhaps life would have taken a different turn. But we all find ourselves locked into the decisions we made decades ago, with little logical rationale to back them up, just hope. We lose control of our destiny.

In contrast, the author's all-powerful role means you can make your characters do anything you want. However, interacting with people from many cultures, I have come to realise that human psychology is the same everywhere – there are boundaries you cannot cross regarding human behaviour. Behaviours must be credible, even though some quite extraordinary things can happen and remain believable within the boundaries of the human personality. Hence the anxiety of a young British engineer, the frustration of a middle-aged lonely American, the joy of an Arab teenager and the anger of a Greek businessman are all relevant to our own perception of reality.

The nature of reality, consciousness and perception has long been a major preoccupation of mine. This collection explores the perceptions behind human interactions – often those between men and women. Some of the stories were written before the advent of mobile phones, the internet and social media, so the challenges encountered by the protagonists are quite different from those of the Millennial generation. Others are very current.

Several of the stories are beyond our time. They project,

into the future or the past, that universal humanity – its prosaic calm, its everyday concerns, the sudden terror of the unexpected and the slow onset of tragedy. In these pages, you will meet engaging characters with whom you will have some common understanding whether you love them or despise them. You may meet some of them again in a future story collection, or in real life. Like Jonas Jonasson's *The 100-Year-Old Man Who Climbed Out of the Window and Disappeared*, we all have a unique history. Although it may be unknown to those around us, much of it is richly flavoured – comedy and tragedy, fear and pleasure, pain and joy. Being human.

These experiences and emotions emerge in the narratives of our brief existence. I offer some of them to you here. If you laugh, good. If you think, great. If you cry, then you know something of the heart.

Oh, and the O Level? I passed – just.

GRC, Cha Am, Thailand, June 2021

Fares Fair

The rain had stopped for the time being and patches of blue were becoming visible behind the grey cast of the sky. It was a typical spring day in London in the 1980s. The early evening air was fresh. Shafts of sunlight darted across the buildings and played on the damp roadway.

Of the dozen or so travellers waiting at the bus stop there were a couple of schoolgirls, an elderly Sikh gentleman, a skinhead with face tattoos and an Afro-Caribbean mother with three young children. One person, though, radiated a strange attraction, inviting a second glance. She possessed one of those remarkably serene faces usually only associated with cosmetics advertisements set on misty tropical islands. Almost expressionless, but with an air of apparent confidence, she avoided the gaze of the other waiting passengers, profound thoughts flittering from her dark eyes and becoming entangled in the vagaries of the timetable before her. *Don't forget to tender the exact fare* the timetable instructed, as if to one who had failed to grasp an important question.

The careful observer might have noticed the suspicion of a smile grace her features as the bus drew up and the rear platform of the old vehicle aligned with the queue. The conductor leaned out to beckon the passengers forward. The long hair of the dark-eyed girl fluttered in the breeze and the litter scattered on the pavement stood up and danced. The small crowd moved forward, and others joined at the last moment. She mounted the platform first, for who would stand in the way of such a face. Carrying her fashionable shopping basket, she moved easily to the front of the crowded bus and sat down in the front seat on the left next to a young man in a grey suit. She liked looking forward at the road over the bonnet of the bus. The young man glanced at her as she took her place and took every opportunity to look round again as the journey commenced.

The inside of a London omnibus is a sacred theatre in which only certain players are permitted major speaking parts. The young man and the girl were mere extras with two scripted lines apiece – "£1.20 please" and "Thank you very much." These lines were uttered in response to the familiar cues delivered by the conductor, the well-known leading actor,

"Have your fares ready, ladies and gentlemen—Where to, luv?"

The girl received her ticket and said, "Thank you very much," with warm tones and an upward glance at the conductor that would have conjured applause from the audience at the Old Vic. Here, however, her only audience was the young man, who, had he dared, would have dearly loved to applaud. He gave the impression that he felt inadequate to play next to an actress of this calibre and he fluffed his lines.

"Well?" asked the leading man.

"Er…£1.20, please," said the young man too loudly, as he clumsily handed over only a pound coin, reaching across the girl to the conductor standing in the aisle. "Sorry, I was distracted…" he said nervously, as he fumbled in his pocket for more change. The leading man grimaced. That line was not in the script and extemporisation was not appreciated – it was like making unscriptural additions to the prayer book.

Painstakingly balancing himself against the driver's sudden acceleration, the conductor counted out change from his satchel and handed it over to the young man. Again, subconsciously scene-stealing, the young man fumbled and dropped two or three coins. They fell into the girl's open shopping basket, clattering against a tin of beans.

"Oh, I'm so sorry," he exclaimed, as the leading man left the disrupted scene in disgust and moved on to Act 2 and a more competent cast.

"I'm being rather clumsy today." He leaned over to retrieve the coins. She dug them out and handed them back to him. The ice had been broken.

"It's raining." A predictable opening line of a seemingly trivial nature for a conversation in London, although more appropriate for a provincial theatre production than the West End. The girl smiled politely, placing her newspaper over the basket. Now the money had been recovered, she was content to make conversation with this repertory novice, even though he had failed to gain the respect of the more experienced players.

Naturally, the conversation was a little superficial, as at parties when strangers are thrown together: "You must meet Bill and Fiona – wonderful people." It's curious, isn't it? That people never have a neutral reaction to each other. You either vaguely like someone or vaguely dislike them or are suspicious of them when you first meet. The impression can change quickly over the course of a five-minute conversation, but that first impression remains. And so it was with this couple, who were by no means a couple. They were OK about each other. They felt no hostility, only vague acceptance. She thought he was harmless, if a bit too Cockney. He felt a little sad about her – a shame really.

They spoke of the weather, the cost of living and their respective jobs. He was an assistant at a travel agency. Though a little evasive, she was some kind of dealer in coins and medals.

He spoke of his boss and his low pay – he could never afford most of the holidays he sold and he was always afraid of making some dreadful mistake – Monaco, Malaga, they all sounded the same, didn't they? She asked him about the exotic places he marketed but never visited. In some cases, his knowledge was remarkable and, he admitted, first-hand. The company had sent him on one or two trips to meet local representatives on the ground, to encourage the off-season traveller, that kind of thing.

She, too, travelled. Just travelled. She didn't specify the destinations in her conversation nor, indeed, in the darkness of her eyes. Elusive, mysterious, yet somehow completely at home in her skin. She might have had some unknown rendezvous – with a diamond dealer in Amsterdam or an Italian fashion designer in Milan. Those were her people, thought the young man with the second-hand air tickets. He wondered what was really behind that face, those eyes, that caused him to pour out his thoughts while she told him nothing of herself and let no thread of her being find its way into his hands.

The psychologists who designed the seats of London's classic Routemaster bus were ahead of their time. They are too narrow for two average-sized people to sit next to one another without coming into contact, but just too wide for the contact to be at all cosy. The result was that two passengers could experience the warmth of a stranger's body without sharing the warmth of their mind, their soul and their feelings. Although the young man had been able to engage his travelling companion in conversation and drink in the aroma of her perfume, he could not discern her heart, which seemed resolutely locked away forever. He experienced a fleeting melancholy that reflected his uncomfortable situation.

He felt frustration that such uncomplicated human contact could only be temporary – a fleeting relationship on a bus, over a desk in the agency, in the street or cinema queue, meeting hundreds of people but, in reality, none. He would like to have continued this relationship at a later time but, as usual, his trade got in the way. In any case, he thought it most unlikely that his temporary companion was the type of person who commenced deep friendships on London buses. Most likely her closest acquaintances were people she knew from her mysterious business dealings, or met at smart parties or intellectual soirees at sophisticated art galleries.

Art nouveau, however, was not at the forefront of her consciousness at that moment. It would be mistaken to say that she was nervous or even particularly ill at ease, but she felt a certain disquiet at the continued presence of this young man, as if she knew something that would anger him if she inadvertently mentioned it. She had hoped he would get off sooner as they were in the fare zone by now. She could not get off early. It would be too obvious – she had the same fare as he did, although she had boarded a stop later. So, the conversation continued.

It was just as well that his tales of the travel agency seemed to be inexhaustible, since she did not particularly wish to discuss the details of her work with him. It was too complicated, he wouldn't understand and, indeed, wouldn't wish to if he really followed what she could tell him.

The bus lurched to a stop at traffic lights and her newspaper fell to the floor from the top of her shopping basket. The young man bent to pick it up. A vestige of chivalry still remains in the male mind, even the mind of this man, whose transactional way of life seemed to preclude such considerations. He replaced the newspaper on top of her basket as she looked through the window towards the bus driver reading the *Motoring News* while waiting for the lights. She turned back to the young man and thanked him.

As the lights changed, the young man looked at his watch and continued the conversation, exclaiming about the slow passage of time on the homeward journey, which always seemed at least three times as long as the journey to work. She agreed and managed the suspicion of a smile, which was a little more than she had previously allowed to escape from her placid face. When she glanced across him to the window on the left, she saw that she was not far from her destination. But as she waited for his next remark, she realised he had stood up and was about to make his way past her. She stood to let him by, holding on to her basket and feeling a certain relief that they would not alight at the same stop.

They exchanged goodbyes in a friendly manner as he tripped over her foot.

"Sorry, I am being a clumsy git today," he said, smiling broadly.

"See you," she replied, with no intention of letting that happen.

He looked round once more and smiled, a little sheepishly, she thought, as he made his way back along the bus past passengers of all shapes and sizes crowding the seats and the aisle. She could see he had reached the platform as the bus chugged to a halt.

The bus pulled away and turned slowly to the right as the girl slid into the vacant seat by the window. She briefly looked into her shopping basket and checked on the young man's wallet which she had deftly grasped and slid into the basket while he was rescuing her newspaper. She was relieved that he had gone and taken his cheerful Cockney banter with him. But somehow, she felt quite warm about their little conversation. He was not such a bad guy – pity he had to be a mark.

The young man hopped off the bus as it drew to a halt and

moved rapidly away in the opposite direction, striding deliberately to put in plenty of distance.

"Easy." He grinned as he walked on and fingered her purse in his pocket. He could feel the credit cards – it was going to be a good evening.

September 1982

Someone Else's Gods

The Gods of Mount Olympus were like Superman, Batman and Catwoman, only not as good. Morally good, I mean. They were every bit as swashbuckling and generally got up to more interesting things. The Gods of America, you see – Batman and those Marvel characters that I never got to grips with and the fundamentalist gods of the born again – they're someone else's gods. Second-hand gods. But the Gods of Olympus – well they were your real gods, weren't they? I mean not real real, if you see what I mean. Just well, real. What gods should be like. With faults. They didn't equate religion with morality in the way the Catholics or the Americans do. Or with heavenly reward as the Muslims do. Religion for the ancient Greeks was about now, about earthy things – that battle, that oracle, that woman; this woman.

How a country with no health service and no gun control can go on about morality, I don't understand. But then, who understands other people's gods? Capitalism and guns – they are gods too. Who was it said the right to bear arms is only slightly less ludicrous than the right to arm bears? I've seen bears up close you know. Seen them. Seen their eyes in the torchlight. Never seen a gun up close, not pointed at me anyway. Seen Poseidon up close, though, in a force 9 outside Milos on Christmas Eve. Call that a storm? This is a storm!

You see, I always thought I had faith. But I didn't have faith, I had belief…and I had fear. Fear of God – no problem, got plenty of that. The devils believe, and shudder. I know where they're coming from. I shuddered. Does that mean I was a devil? I didn't think so. I was a good man then. Of course, when you're young it's easy to be good and have a clean conscience. You can repent and get back to zero sin. But there comes a point when the odd bits start to build up and you can't seem to get rid of them, and then you can't remember what it is you were going to repent. But there I go again, equating religion with morality. If I hadn't done that…no, no. No *ifs*. This is now. It can be different.

When I went to those rallies, those meetings, sang hymns, said prayers, it was immediate. It was now. But there was a screwing up of my eyes, a holding of breath, a denying of something in my head. A holding back – a suspension of disbelief. All these people thought it was true and they told you what risk of hell you had if you didn't believe it and if you didn't accept forgiveness. Well, I could understand that. I needed forgiveness even though I was a good person. I mean, there were evil thoughts. Well, that was the trouble – they were nice thoughts actually. There was the one where the girl wearing a white shirt over black underwear comes into the room and starts undoing the shirt and…but I digress.

My wife – Jen, my ex-wife I mean – she said I was mean. And she's right. But is that a sin? Is it an evil thought to think about not giving a full 10% tip? I didn't get a coin out to give to that old woman – *next time*, I said to myself. But what if she froze to death that night like Tiny Tim? What then? It's on my conscience.

Jen said I had betrayed her. She was right of course. I betrayed her because she rejected me.

Or so I thought.

I needed someone who would hold me in the night. Not just the intimate, wild stuff. Not just that. And she wouldn't talk about it. I thought she was about to walk out with one of her money-market friends. Hooray Henrys or barrow boys – maybe both, but I suppose you can't be both really. But then they would call her up early in the morning in the hotel to discuss the day's conference proceedings. She'd go to one of their rooms, as requested, and they'd open the door to her naked. She thought it was a laugh. Was betraying her a sin? Yes, of course it was. I just wanted to be happy, but I wasn't – not after betraying her.

So, you get to the stage when you know you can never be happy. Not with all those gods looking over you. Someone else's gods mainly. They're just there. Looking over you. Tut-tutting or urging you on. No, I don't hear voices, if that's what you're thinking. They're not voices. They make you think you should go that way, don't cross the road here, cross it there. They just won't let you have any peace. No joy. No joy any more. The gods absorb it all. If you play along with them and do something they really like – make a sacrifice or something – then you get some. They let you have a tiny bite of joy once in a while. Makes you think it's worth going on.

I know I'm mad. I have insight into my condition. I know it doesn't really matter if I don't count in fives, or if I don't put the cup straight on the table five times, or ten or fifteen. If I don't get it right. Sometimes you'll see me bobbing up and down trying to get it just right – how I'm walking, putting something down, turning a page. And reading is really hard. I have to take my eyes off the right letters when I turn the page. And the right words. Not some awful word like *murder* or *betrayal* or *hell*. Not some letter like *D* which might stand for Dad, because then something might happen to Dad. Or *M* for Mum. But she's dead now, so perhaps that doesn't matter any more, but then, who knows if she's somewhere with some devil punching her every time I take my eyes off the page on the letter *M*. You don't know, do you, if any of this really matters? What are all those gods doing? The ones that might have her held in a cave somewhere. Those Gods on Olympus. Because once you start believing in gods there's no end to what they might do to you.

I know I'm mad, but it's how I feel that hurts. Doesn't matter that I can think straight. I can't feel straight. Is it them that make me feel like that? The Gods? There's no saying what someone else's gods are doing to you. What they're thinking, plotting around their fires in lofted halls. They're not generally very friendly with me, so they don't tell me. I've never found a friendly one yet. That's why I'm always on the outside. Other people are friendly with the gods, or at least they say they are, which is a lot easier. But not me. They all seem very frightening and unpredictable.

Poseidon's not the worst of them. There's that Ares. You know he actually encourages war? I bet he's behind the gun lobby. No, I can't bet. I might bet my soul by accident. As it pops out, there will be some god there to catch it and run off with it. And then I would be soul-less. And I would not care what I did and I would have no conscience about it. And despite having no conscience, I would not be depressed all the time any more and I would be like a bank robber – like Bonnie and Clyde or Butch and Sundance – ready to laugh it off and spend the loot happily and not care who I had killed in the process.

But I didn't kill her – Jen, I mean. I just betrayed her. And now she's dead. But I don't feel bad about that, personally, I mean, because really that wasn't my fault because I was always very, very careful about not taking my eyes off the page while I was looking at the letter *J*.

Dionysus is a bit friendly. He doesn't mind a laugh, old Dionysus, and him a son of Zeus, who's really a bit strict. Except of course that Zeus went round having it off with lots of lovely ladies and siring children. Children like Dionysus. Dionysus likes wine – he invented it. And sex. Well, all the gods do – wine and sex for themselves, even if they don't like us doing it.

The Goddess, though. She's in with Dionysus. Chaos, fertility rites. I'm sorry I never got to go to a fertility rite. It's hard to find out where they hold them. But then I wouldn't have enjoyed it because of the fears. I would have had to put the wine cup down straight and the girls would have got fed up waiting. But the Goddess, she was all right. She gave us some love. Maybe that's why the Americans don't like her. Don't like sex at all. Look what happened to Larry Flynt. How can they have all that violence in films and yet, one nice explicit bed scene and they're all up in arms. Real arms sometimes, and they say it's for God. Someone else's god. Not mine. What is mine?

So, I feel different now. Here in the dark. In the isolation cell…I feel so much better. I've done something for her…for them. All of them. I reckon some of the Gods were pleased because I did what they asked. I feel joy, because I know I've done something not just for the Gods, but something to get back at other people's gods for what they made those people do to me. And her. Soon I will die and then I won't have to worry about any of it. And if there are gods? But no. I killed them all when I did it. It was so much easier than I'd expected. The main thing was not to be caught with the weapon. So easy. Just bought it in a shop. Hardly any questions. They liked my accent, joked about it. I gave some plausible story about being a journalist wanting to see how easy it was to buy one – an Uzi. They made it as easy as pie, piece of piss, falling off a… He made it easy, I should say. He and his cronies who stopped the ban on assault weapons being renewed. Sow the wind. Reap the whirlwind.

I didn't think it would be easy to get near though. That was a surprise. Like the guy in the Batman costume who scaled the walls of Buckingham Palace. I just walked along Pennsylvania Avenue, waited by the fence opposite the nuclear protest bloke. Saw him come across the lawn and I fired into the crowd when I saw him. I'd been watching of course. Knew the programme – it's all on the net.

"That's for Jen," I shouted, and the press got it wrong of course. Thought I said Ken. 'Course not. Mind you, I always had great respect for Mr Livingstone – almost as mad as me. Though, of course, he went up in the same explosion that devastated London. He and 50,000 others. But it was Jen I thought of when I heard. Even though we'd been apart five years and I had been dead most of that time, effectively. Spent most days counting, putting my coat on right, pulling my socks on and off a hundred times before it was right. It's like the Gods in the trees and the water. You have to please them or something terrible will happen.

They make you do it, those Gods. You must sacrifice the most precious thing you have – time.

April 2005

Ordering Pizza Has Never Been So Much Fun

When Simon invited me to a business meeting, I thought it was going to be another attempt to get me to join a pyramid selling scheme for water softeners. But it was a free lunch at one of my favourite pizza parlours on Clarke Quay, Singapore's trendiest waterfront, so why not? If I could get him off water softeners and onto the phone number of that girl who works with him in the finance department at Armstrong Baker Mollis Trivet Watterson and Zogbi, the venture capital boutique, it could be time well spent.

After the first pleasantries and making our orders – his, a meat lover's, mine, vegetarian – he went immediately on the attack, saying that I wasn't going to believe this, but ordering pizza had never been so much fun. And I could be a big part of it (!).

"It's very simple. You see, Mike, in M-Theory, the universe has ten space dimensions – not just the three we can see, and the time dimension that we can't see. So, our 3D + time universe is, in fact, a portion of an actual universe trapped by the vibration modes of its strings in such a way that no electromagnetic information can pass from or to, the other dimensions. However, gravitational energy can pass through, so we can detect leakage of gravitational energy from or to the other dimensions and, thus, experimentally demonstrate their existence."

"Er…" I said.

The image of the black-haired girl at Armstrong Baker Mollis

Trivet Watterson and Zogbi spun before my eyes. She was slim but well-endowed, not too tall, with the cutest smile, which she had directed at me more than once and I thought that maybe I...

"So that's how it's done," continued Simon. "We simply send the order, they convert the pizza into a gravitational wave and deliver it via the ninth dimension that just happens to have the best parameters for maintaining most of the flavours. Although it does have an annoying tendency to make meat come out blue."

This was not entirely within my field of competence, so I had a few questions. Prosaic ones maybe but, you know. And the raven-haired beauty was really the focus of my quest today, rather than gravitational waves from the ninth dimension. But I would have to be patient and find an opening.

"Wait, wait. You're losing me at the first hurdle. What is this? Pizza delivery from the ninth dimension? Excuse me if I seem a little out of my depth. I'm basically just a kitchen equipment manufacturer with sidelines in white goods and industrial catering – also keys cut."

"Sorry, Mike, I realise it's a bit heavy. I should have taken it slower, but I'm just so excited by this. You see, we have no trouble these days doing everything over the net and over the airwaves. Anything to do with information we can do remotely – e-books, money transfers and so on. We don't have to meet anyone any more except to socialise and of course to do deals where the face-to-face stuff counts."

I could think of one or two other situations where being face to face counts and, indeed, many other positions, but I let that go. He went on.

"So, you see, to cut a long story short. We have worked out how to deliver physical objects over the air – not to put too fine a point on it – pizza! It's what everyone wants, and how tedious it is to have to call for delivery and wait thirty minutes when you want it right now!"

I feel somewhat sorry for those whose carnal appetites demand to be satisfied that quickly, but never mind.

"But my partners – the suppliers, as it were – want to expand the deal they're doing and think that an organisation like yours is just the vehicle for a global delivery enterprise."

In my experience, propositions that sound too good to be true usually are, but I was intrigued enough to let him continue and, anyway, the pizzas had arrived. Remarkably quickly, it struck me. I thought he looked slightly odd for a couple of seconds – couldn't quite put my finger on it. He started to say something, but I cut him off as I wasn't ready for another sales pitch just yet.

"So, how did you contact these people – can I call them people – in, what did you say, the ninth dimension? What are they like?"

"Well, it was an accident really. One of those quantum fluctuations everyone talks about."

As far as I am aware I don't often talk about quantum fluctuations, but there we are. I guess I'm behind the times even though I can use Facebook, admire pictures of pretty pussycats, and get into violent arguments with complete strangers.

"I was working on some strategic planning papers for the pizza parlour, you see. It was late."

Yes, I always work late on strategic papers, it makes them seem more plausible. Especially when red wine is involved. In the morning things may look different.

"So, you were contacted by creatures from a different dimension?"

"Sort of – well several different dimensions really – you see where we use length, breadth, height and time, they use stuff like crumpledness, stretchiness, extensiveness and glotch. At least that's the best I can convey them in English."

"I'm not familiar with glotch. Can you elucidate?" My tone must have seemed a little frivolous.

"No, not really – but I suppose the best way to describe it is that it's sort of like a woolly cardigan that's been through the wash too many times and all the knots have curled up with little fringes hanging off. Well, if you looked at the fringes under a microscope with ultraviolet light, that would be a bit like glotch. But don't ask me about swettlishness."

"I see," I said, though I didn't, and I had no intention of following up on the swettlishness dimension – no joke intended. This was 99% incredible. But I did notice that the pizza sitting in front of him had blue pepperoni on it.

"Tell me more. How does all this work? And what exactly is the proposition you have for me?"

I noticed it more clearly this time – he had suddenly become slightly blurred. As if I had taken my glasses off. I wiped my eyes and he seemed to be back in focus.

"Ah, they have given me some information for you."

"What? You mean the creatures from the ninth dimension?"

"I don't think you should call them that. It sounds like B-movie science fiction. They can be a bit sensitive."

"Sorry. So, you have insight into their personal feelings then?"

"Well, it's not so much that I have insight, but that the universe has insight. You see, we are just knots of low entropy in the fabric of a universal consciousness."

I did not take the bait – a lesson in Buddhist philosophy

and thermodynamics was not on the agenda. What I was really trying to do was work out how to mention, subtly, my interest in the truly and seriously delightful girl in his finance department.

"So, what are they telling you?" I continued, feigning both interest and credulity.

"Just that this is a great opportunity for us – you and me – to make a huge pot of money before other operators get in on the act."

"Right. Kind of first mover advantage? In fact, pan-dimensional first mover advantage."

"Exactly."

He became blurry again for an instant. I really must stop taking those slimming pills. I continued, "But isn't it usually true that it's the second or third mover that makes the money? Look at poor old Garry what's 'is name at Digital Research – nobody remembers who he is. And Bill Gates is the richest man in the world."

"I get your meaning. And all due respect to Bill, but in the ninth dimension – or rather the sixth to tenth dimensions – experience in corporate strategy has some different characteristics."

"I see," I said. Damn! I'd done it again. But I had picked up something and I had to respond.

"Didn't you say sixth to tenth? Do you mean they operate in five dimensions, not four like us?"

"Ah well spotted – yes indeed. That's where swettlishness comes in and that's what makes it easier for them to manage telekinesis properly…you know, transferring physical objects by manipulating the gravity waves."

"Of course, that extra dimension makes all the difference."

"Indeed, it does! You see, while we can only get information to them on the gravity conveyor, they can send back physical objects to us. It's like pan-dimensional 3D printing."

Ah, now here was something I had actually heard of. Last year, 3D printing was being heralded as a fundamental revolution in manufacturing. Now you can get a machine to lay down the detailed structure of an object just from a computer program – a set of information about the structure – and the printer – fed with the right material – will do the rest. We had done it in the lab with plastic machine parts. Maybe this was starting to sound kind of plausible. But 3D printing of perishables? Especially fresh, hot and tasty ones with extra toppings of your choice was a little way beyond state of the art, human-wise.

For a moment, he went blurry again. I took another slice of pizza. It was delicious, so no quality issues then.

He continued, as if he had just been cued by a prompter.

"And you should be aware that the opportunities for manufacturing the delivery devices are huge."

"Well. If it works, it could be infinite," I replied cautiously, knowing that the concept of infinity is not something one should bat around lightly over a fast-food lunch. But how many pizza restaurants are there in the world…?

"So, we want you to be a part of it, and the opportunity is only open now. I will be going to several other likely prospects if you don't give us the thumbs up at this meeting."

Ah, so now the familiar pyramid salesman's hard sell. I was used to this and had many methods of countering it, the main one being that, at my time of life, I just didn't bloody care. And really – the credibility side was pretty stretched.

He really did become blurry this time and he could see that I had noticed. It lasted a good thirty seconds – like a small earth tremor.

"They are not too pleased that you are so hesitant," Simon said, looking nervous.

I thought I had been utterly poker-faced actually, so what did they know about what was going on inside my head? Strange. Now come on – what is this? I was getting drawn in too far.

"No, Simon. Sorry. Not right now, mate. I'm too far on in this game to be cornered into fast decisions I might regret. You know me." I suddenly remembered the girl in finance and felt a rush of adrenaline. "You'll have to give me time to think about this. I'll need a lab demo, need to do some costs and benefits, get the spreadsheet guys onto it. Not something you can just snap up on the off chance. Especially as 90% of me doesn't believe a word of it!"

What happened next is still not very clear to me. My pizza vanished before my eyes. The plate was still there, but every last crumb had gone. And there was a bizarre empty feeling in my stomach – like I hadn't eaten anything since breakfast.

Simon looked a bit sad and embarrassed, but he did not seem surprised about the vanishing pizza.

"They've gone offline. I hope you haven't wrecked this for me."

I was a bit speechless but managed to form a suitable platitude and try to change the subject.

"Well, I'm sure they'll be back – now, about that rather gorgeous girl in your finance department..."

"Not in the mood now, Mike. Sorry and all that, but I have to rush back to the office."

As he headed for the door, his pizza, I noticed, was still there unfinished. Although I was feeling a bit stunned, curiosity got the better of me. I cautiously reached out and took a piece of the blue pepperoni. It tasted great – well balanced, spicy, but not too spicy, and not too oily. A great product.

I felt odd for a second and a thought suddenly popped into my head, *Missed a good one there, Mike,* as a vivid three-dimensional image of the girl in the finance department at Armstrong Baker Mollis Trivet Watterson and Zogbi danced before my eyes. I distinctly saw her wink at me, thus shattering every illusion I had about the nature of reality.

There really is no such thing as a free lunch.

December 2012 – written just after the Mayan calendar ended. We're still here I notice.

The Optician of Szeged

Human life is a complex interfacing of the stories of hundreds or thousands of people, and it becomes less clearly defined the older you get and the more experiences you have with an ever-expanding set of interlocutors – family, colleagues, acquaintances, friends, lovers and enemies, or at least people you would rather not see again in or out of a dark alley. Which brings me to the deceptive game of love, where events and protagonists may not be what they seem.

The honey trap is a standard plot for spy stories. An attractive woman uses her seductive charms to get information, a confession or a plan from her victim. Or sets him up for blackmail or assassination. Our senses are both intrigued and horrified as we are brought up from the cradle to believe in the nurturing and comforting role of women. For the male of the species, after all, mother is the protector of and provider for the little boy who lives within all men. Well, maybe not Genghis Khan – his teddy bear has never been found.

And so, as I tell you a story about female schemes, don't let me put you off your mother. But you may want to look more carefully at the object of desire that inhabits your bed, or your fantasies.

Meeting someone in the street may not be a good start. Claudia Kovacs is a good example. Claudia plays to the male fantasy that he is attractive and plays it well. Our hero, let us call him Martin, walks out of a restaurant onto a pedestrian street busy with shoppers. It is early evening in September, warm and pleasant, although Martin is somewhat dissatisfied with his day. Meetings did not go as well as planned and, to top it all, the meal was disappointing and the wine undrinkable. The city is Budapest, one of his favourite places, but all he has to look forward to tonight is a book on marketing strategy and some preparation for tomorrow. He doesn't plan to go out anywhere.

So, as he walks quickly out of the restaurant into the pedestrian boulevard, fiddling with his mobile, he is surprised to walk straight into an attractive blonde woman who drops her bag as he cannons into her. Gentleman that he is, Martin picks up the bag and the woman quickly engages him in conversation. Martin does not see this as odd – although he should. As he is an obvious Englishman, it is not unusual for him to be engaged in random conversations in a foreign city. The British generate a strange allure – curious, over-confident, organised and ambitious people still travelling the world with the prime intention of explaining to foreigners what they are doing wrong.

Claudia looks at her watch (gold – always impressive) and declares that she has to meet her mother in an hour to go to a concert, but why don't they have a drink? Of course, Martin is flattered and delighted to be drawn out of his sombre mood. Claudia just happens to know a nice place nearby.

They sit close together in a corner seat – plush velour – and order a drink; he a red wine and she a white. The band begins to play – incongruously, just as in 'Yellow Submarine'. Claudia is a great conversationalist, with almost faultless English. She is an optician, from Szeged, a sizeable town in the south of Hungary. She and her mother are in town for a series of Spanish guitar concerts. It's all quite intellectual and Martin is absorbed. He thinks she is very good looking, with all the right attributes –

nice full hairstyle, pretty face, slim but good figure. Attractive, intellectual, eloquent and she has a good job. The obvious question is looming – *Is your partner here as well?*

Their drinks arrive. The red is good, a Prince Mircea from Romania. Strong, full-bodied with just a hint of cinnamon and blackberry. Yes, he actually says that, with one eyebrow raised, and she giggles. Her white wine is a quarter bottle of champagne – Veuve Clicquot.

"Ah, you are a fan of the widow," he says, grinning.

She doesn't get that one and he explains. She nods appreciatively and they clink glasses and sip. His previous question has conveniently evaporated in the heat of the moment. It is time for hers.

"Do you dance?" she asks, leaning in more closely as the volume of the music reaches a crescendo.

"Yes, I do a bit," he replies, remembering that he broke the ice with both his ex-wives on the dance floor.

As they stand up, she is taller than he thought. Unexpectedly she takes his hand briefly to lead him onto the small dance floor. At this point it might have been sensible to ask what has happened to her mother. But it does not occur to him or, if subliminally, his unconscious mental processes manage to shrug it off, sensing perhaps in their evolutionary fervour a potential opportunity for the distribution of genetic material.

The second song is 'Sultans of Swing', one of Martin's all-time favourites. He knows all the words. Martin's daytime job is drifting far from his thoughts as he croons the lyrics into Claudia's ear. She seems suitably impressed and he leads her back to the table at the end of the song.

It occurs to him, as she goes off to the ladies', that he is getting a little merry and he remembers that he has already swallowed a couple of sherries and a glass of the undrinkable wine earlier. He notices that she has dispatched the champagne, or at least that the bottle is empty, although he can't actually recall seeing her drink it.

Nevertheless, when she returns, he orders another round. Mother, it turns out, has gone back to their hotel with a headache.

"So, we have the whole evening."

They chat for a while longer, mainly about his work and the conference he is due to address in two days' time. He tries to ask some small things about the varifocal lenses he is thinking of getting now that he has the joy of being both short-sighted and long-sighted at the same time, but she doesn't pick up on it. Probably doesn't want to talk shop on a night like this.

They get halfway through the second drink when the band starts to play 'Strangers in the Night'. She turns confidentially and smiles.

"Come on," she says and glides out onto the dance floor where several couples are already in clinches swaying to the music.

It's pretty full on. His hand caresses her back and hers goes round his shoulder. Her other hand folds into his grip against his chest. Her head is on his shoulder and her perfumed hair on the side of his face. He suddenly realises that he would give up both of his semi-serious girlfriends for this one.

As Sinatra's warm tones consider the chances of love, Martin suddenly realises it's gone from less than 20% to better than evens. They walk back to the table hand-in-hand. He gives her an appraising look as they sit down, and she smiles warmly.

"Why don't we go somewhere a bit quieter?" she suggests confidentially.

"Why not? I'll get the bill." Again, the gentleman. He won't hear of her paying, although he is a little taken aback that the bill for four drinks and some crisps is the equivalent of €200. He flips his MasterCard onto the table, whence it is whisked away and returned five minutes later with a slip to sign and – unusually for this city – a PIN pad (for extra security, they tell him).

At this point, it's worth considering the unconscious mental processes once more. Martin is getting hooked, but he is fully aware of this. He can see that he has been grossly overcharged and that it has something to do with Claudia. But she is just so… nice! And he is having the best evening he has had for months and…so, what the hell! If it's a complete fantasy and he wakes up tomorrow with a sore head and a series of fraudulent credit card transactions, so what? It is a mystery to men how we can be simultaneously taken in and not taken in. What is the deal in a relationship, anyway? There must be give and take, but who is doing which more of the time?

The second place is much like the first but, as predicted, quieter. The conversation continues – relaxed, fluent, not touching too much on areas of real emotion. Do you like this film, that artist? She does know about Spanish guitar virtuosos – she knows where Paco Pena has been playing recently and she has heard of Julian Bream. Also, she likes the compositions of Heitor Villa-Lobos, and can name some of them. There is a depth of sincerity that is hard to see through. If he is just a mark, Martin thinks, she is remarkably well-informed about what he would want to talk about. But, on the other hand, when is the last time he had a conversation about Spanish guitar virtuosos? Maybe she is just leading his mind – like a conjuror – down exactly the paths she wants it to go. She is fully in control but has that extraordinary knack of giving the impression that he is taking the lead. Like a mother encouraging her precious child out into the world.

They dance again and sit down to a second round of drinks.

And then one inconsistency, one chink in the armour. One second thought. She lays her head on his shoulder for a few seconds and sighs. It is over almost before he notices, but the atmosphere has subtly changed. She has lost the initiative.

He takes over.

"Let's go," he says gently. He pays another gigantic bill. No PIN pad this time. They walk together arm-in-arm towards the Danube. It is midnight, but the river is busy. He has no expectations, just unconscious hopes. He hopes for a kiss. If there is a kiss, there will be something more. But it does not happen. She has regained control as the cool night air awakes her professional skills.

They gaze at the river for a while. He has to say it, staring ahead at the reflections of the lights of the Buda Palace on the water, "You know I'd like you to come back to the hotel with me."

"I know," she says and looks at him warmly with those cool blue eyes. "But not this time." Naturally, and without a word, they move away from the railings, past the little dog statues, back towards Vörösmarty Tér and the end of the evening.

"I would very much like to see you again," he begins, as he ushers her towards the taxi rank.

"Me too."

They exchange numbers and a chaste kiss on both cheeks. Then they arrange to meet for lunch the next day, in his hotel bar, at 12.30.

"Bye for now," she says, stepping elegantly into the taxi.

Back in his room, he checks his emails and Googles her – optician, Szeged, Kovacs. And there she is. No picture, but a description – the right age and qualifications. His confidence is buoyed up. His doubts are quieted, and he replays the evening in his mind, somehow glossing over his previous suspicions. He undresses and lays down, wondering what it would have been like if she had accepted his invitation as they stood by the river. He is soon asleep and sleeps soundly. When he wakes, he feels a little groggy; happy, but more circumspect about what is going on.

*

A couple of meetings in the morning pass quickly. He is preoccupied but concentrating hard. He is back at the hotel before noon. He smartens up and goes down to the bar at 12.20. Time passes inconceivably slowly. 12.23 – he orders a gin and tonic, 12.27 – it arrives, but she doesn't. 12.35 – he will call her in five minutes. 12.40 – he will call her in five minutes. He doesn't.

By one o'clock, he is resigned to it. It's up to her after all – she is a free agent; she can exercise her free will. Maybe she has changed her mind about seeing him again. Maybe it was, indeed, as he really knew all along, just a scam. After struggling with himself and his mobile, he makes the call. An old lady answers. She doesn't speak English. The mother maybe? He asks for Claudia – Claudia Kovacs. Incomprehensible Hungarian. She puts the phone down… He waits another half-hour before the light, which had already dawned early yesterday evening with the first bill, dawns decisively and finally. Then he summons the waitress and orders comfort food – fish and chips – and relapses into a grim mood.

Six months later, the credit card fraud begins. Fortunately, he spots it after the first half dozen withdrawals from an ATM in Kiev. $3,000, gone over a weekend, when his bank helpfully does not update on-line balances. So, the crime was not just organised, but ultra-efficiently organised. *How many, Claudia?* he thinks to himself. And then: *How many Claudias?* A double whammy – emotional and financial, a network of broken hearts and plundered bank balances.

*

"Hey." A happy voice with a slight *Mittel Europa* accent wakes him from his depressing reverie as he pushes the fish and chips round the plate. "So sorry to be so late. I hope you didn't think I wasn't coming."

He jumps up, the chair crashes to the floor. They embrace. She takes the initiative and kisses him full on the lips – for more than a moment. Six months later, he has spent €15,000 on her – travel, gold, a holiday in Istanbul, a small investment in new equipment for her business. Who knows where the romance will go now? But they are both happy for the moment, even though they cannot be together more than a week a month – until they get things sorted out. What they are doing the rest of the time, they studiously do not probe too much. Maybe she is a charming gangster after all? Maybe he is an inveterate womaniser with no intention of settling in Szeged with an optician? We call this *going out, in a relationship* as Facebook would put it.

*

So, what really happened that lunchtime in his hotel bar in Budapest? Were two people exerting their free will to fall in love? Was one – or both – of them playing two sides against the middle. Was the rendezvous in the bar indeed missed – a straight standing up and letting down? We will never know. It is just a story. Claudia and Martin – never mind their other names – do not exist in reality. Although many people exist who have had their experiences. Being conned, being loved, being both at once.

Even for ourselves, we can never be sure what our ego or id-driven brain processes are up to, pursuing their own agendas. Sometimes conscious, sometimes not. A battle of advantages is going on outside our knowledge, but inside our heads. She says one thing, but unconsciously knows it will convey something

43

more or maybe something different to his unconscious steersman. He promises a little, but she takes it as eternal commitment and designs the curtains in the nursery as she lies back in bed contented and fulfilled, if a little sore.

We call it free will. But is it free and is it will? For Claudia, it is perhaps a lucrative game, the outcome of which she already knows. Martin would have known the outcome too, if he had not been too loaded with testosterone and Prince Mircea to notice. And which Claudia was the more honest?

Could she sleep that night? For Martin, there was no guilt – he slept fine. For Claudia, maybe the ghost of a stirring from the depths that if she had been different and Martin had been different and this city had been different, maybe things could have been different. And so, she kept the date.

But it's just a job, isn't it? That's what she calls it. The game that men and women have been playing for a million years. So, Claudia, when you see yourself in this story, whether or not your name has been changed to protect the innocent, may it make you think for a moment. What will you think? Did you get what you wanted, or did you miss the best opportunity you ever had? The decision is up to you – or whatever is going on in your unconscious mind…

…and mine.

August 2010

It Can't Be Christmas Already?

Dear Darlings!

Well, I can hardly believe it's twelve months since I last put pen to paper, or should I say fingers to the keyboard (!!) to pass on the latest news about me and Dave and the family.

Well!! Where do I start?? It's been an eventful year. Actually, it's been a bloody awful year, but aren't they all (ha, ha). But there have been some bright spots. And some darker ones too! Graham (9 and three quarters (my word processing skills aren't up to doing 'three quarters' properly I'm afraid!! Like in numbers I mean!)) got chicken pox and then passed it on to Dave who, at 37, had a hard time of it. Actually, he was up scratching every night for two weeks!! That's when I decided we should have separate bedrooms. The snoring was bad enough though anyway, and he'd started to smell a bit – but that's old age I guess?!

Anyway, his snoring and smelling didn't turn out to be too much of a problem, because he was able to have quite a delicious affair with his secretary, Monica. I think it started in May, just after I broke mine off with Frank (I think I mentioned him last year – he was such a stud!!).

Anyway, it was a great laugh when I came home early one day and found Dave dressed in Monica's suspenders bent over the kitchen table with a pair of rubber gloves on and a cucumber in his mouth. When I came in, Monica split her sides and the rather cheap camisole she was almost wearing, and we all had a drink and a good gossip! Men will be men!!

But I digress!

In February, we all went skiing and I broke a leg! It was a bit of a downer, as I had to miss two après-ski karaoke nights including the one where they put the lights out and everyone tries to find their other half purely by feel. Such a laugh, especially after six mulled wines. It wouldn't have been too good with a plaster cast though, cos Dave would have found me at the first grope and everyone else would have moved on a bit fast! But never mind, we did meet a very nice Bulgarian couple who put Dave onto some great property deals in Sofia. The bank manager is just coming to terms with that one. We've had to sell the second Ferrari to meet the mortgage payments, as the price sort of shot up at the last moment when we had to avoid being gazumped by a Hungarian speculator. Curiously, it was his wife that Dave ended up with at the après-ski I think.

Anyway, Cheryl (14.3 – decimals are handy really, aren't they!!) has been doing very well at school. And it's a good school too. Approved, actually. I don't understand where education's going to these days really. Though she'd expected to do GSCASCEs or something next year, and apparently, they all pass and then get downgraded at the last minute – heaps of fun!

What a laugh we had this year at the open day when Dave got a little tipsy and told the chairman of the school governors some of his ideas!! I think that may be why they've put us on the list of special advisers. The 'blacklist' Dave says they call it – sounds very important. Until recently, he went to meetings of the blacklist group every month in a pub in Warrington. It was about thirty miles away so he had to stay overnight. I think it was a kind of regional blacklist. Anyway, it gave me a chance to get out with the girls. We'd have such a laugh!! Girls having fun, if you know what I mean??!!

Actually, we've been doing quite a lot of different activities – the discos are good, and the 'pub crawls'!! And the underwear parties are great, only I thought they were actually supposed to sell underwear at them? Barbara (53) just likes us to come round and show her what we've got on and test it for *tactile quality* she says. Sometimes her bloke, Mike (25), joins in and we all have a nice massage with whipped cream and baby oil. It's such a laugh and it's been really good for the slimming.

Then we come to the summer hols. We went back to Malta again. It's nice there. They like the English and they speak it almost. Well, Dave went nuts in the casino and blew a grand one night – bless him!! Course he was too scared to tell me, so he didn't come back to the hotel for three days!!! I eventually found him by chance on a beach round the back of the island with a couple of nice chaps called Julian and Nigel. They were sooo smart and both had those nice little leather caps with chains on them – really cute! We saw a lot of them afterwards, but I think they were a bit shy. At least Julian was when I asked him to do a couple of things for me.

Anyway, me and the kids got on with having a good time while Dave was in his sulk, and we travelled round the island in a hired sports car with another nice friend who's a waiter at the hotel. Miguel his name was. I say *was* because of an unfortunate accident in the lift where he and Dave had a bit of a misunderstanding and a bottle of wine somehow got broken over Miguel's head. The policeman was very nice and said he thought it could all be cleared up quite quickly. I think Dave will only be there for about five years. They tell me there'll be time off for good behaviour – but you know Dave!!

Anyway, so that's why I'm going solo for Christmas this year. Actually, it's not too solo because of Jim who I met at the wife-swapping. It was all arranged for just after the holiday and it seemed a shame not to go after Debbie and Dennis had gone to all that trouble. So, I went along – they always welcome another girl – I guess anyone who can bring a salad is going to go down well anywhere!! Anyway, I met Jim, who's a *financial consultant* – doesn't that sound posh!! So, we got friendly during the evening, and he was really the nicest bloke there apart from Colin who's always such a laugh with the baked beans routine – I think I mentioned that last year.

It turns out that Jim has some great tax deals going, and he told me all about it one day over a bottle or two of champagne in his hotel room. I won't try to explain the details (don't want to give away too much to everyone and, as you know, discretion's my middle name!!) but it seems that if I open an offshore company in the British Virgin Islands, rent the property in Bulgaria to someone from a low tax country in the Middle East and have the proceeds paid into an account in Western Samoa, I can live tax free in Ibiza until Dave gets out. SO that's where I'm writing to you from now!! That's why the funny stamps!!!

Of course, Jim comes over from time to time to help me get things straight, and Cheryl can work in a bar straight away without any GCACSCGEs or whatever. Graham is thrilled and spends all his weekends fishing!! He's been at school here for three months and is starting to speak Spanish (or is it Portuguese??!) really well. I don't understand much at the parents' evenings, but the nice headmaster speaks some English, and he holds my hand whenever I go to see him to give me confidence. Actually, I'm having to see him rather a lot at the moment because of some trouble about Graham, a football boot that got out of control and some damage – something about teeth apparently. Anyway, the headmaster's very helpful, although Jim doesn't seem to like him much.

And I nearly forgot to tell you about Mum (78) and Dad (52). Well, they're still doing OK for their age!! Dad is a bit limited with his sciatica and has to sit in a chair a lot watching TV, and his doctor says he must keep his fluids up, so he has to have plenty of beer. But otherwise, he's quite spritely and his nurse (23) says he's a bit of a handful at times!!

Mum still takes the motorbike out for a spin most days, although she has to watch her step as (and I must have told you this a couple of years back) she lost her licence over the thing with the fish trucks and the fire extinguisher, so she has to avoid getting stopped by the *men in blue*!! Next time it's three years apparently!!! Anyway, not a problem she says, slapping her leather gloves against her thigh, as she does – what a sweetie!! They can never catch up with her in any case, as she knows all the back doubles and can beat them up and down Death Hill when she *brings the turbo thrusters on-line* – all scientific gobbledygook to me, but she knows what she likes after all these years!! I'm happy with just a multiple orgasm from time to time.

So, anyway, must dash. Jim's bringing in a 'paella' from Pedro's round the corner, so I must log off and get ready. I like to look nice for him – he does try so hard! Although this fashion for thongs has its pros and cons if you ask me.

If any of you fancy a break over here, you're welcome – really, very welcome. I mean it. Yes! But after that incident with the brown sauce (that you'll recall from three years back), I do like you to bring your own towels. Just give me a few days' notice so I can clear out the crates from the spare room and rent somewhere temporary for our maid Felicia (18) who usually lives there. I don't know how she gets through so much beer, but she laughs a lot in the afternoons during siesta time so I'm sure she's OK really.

All the best for Christmas and the New Year – don't go getting up to anything I wouldn't!

Love from Samantha, Dave (in absentia!), Cheryl (in the bar!!) and Graham (in trouble!!!) – what a crowd we all are! But it's life, innit??

December 2003

Voices

He'd been doubtful about it all along. Roger Travers thought over his mistake as he glanced out of the window. It was still raining, the wind whipping up white crests on the waves far below the drilling platform, whence he was temporarily exiled by dint of the company's Executive Development Programme. He would be offshore and alone for three months, with the mind-numbing task of analysing operational statistics. Shaking his head, he settled uncomfortably back in his armchair.

There had been three calls already, each one a disappointment. The voices were no good, no good at all. They were either giggly or had what to him were appalling accents – voices without intelligence or sensitivity – one plummy and nasal, one broad Brummy and one a whine. No good at all. They were completely unfeminine, and it had to be someone feminine – not just female.

It wasn't so much being cut off from everyone. Any reasonable female would help to make that more bearable. What was really getting him down was being surrounded by machinery all the time. Cold, untiring machinery. Impressive of course, awesome perhaps, but quite impersonal. You could imagine some kind of mutual appreciation in the old days, a handshake between engineer and machine – the intrepid air-ace in his battered kite, hedge-hopping home, the engineer on a mighty steamship, coaxing his charges into life. But here? Scale and magnificence all right. Plenty of idiosyncratic and perverse behaviour too – the sort of thing that challenges an engineer to relate to the machinery, if it will let him, almost like a romance.

But he was not there to master and control the mighty machines. He was there to take the data they threw at him and make some sense of it. There was something lacking for a person of his skills – it was too remote, not enough for him to do on his own initiative, not enough options about how to run the place, little chance for him to exercise the engineering skills that his university tutor had told him were second to none. No, it was all in the book – the bulky instruction manual for the Platform Central Computer – the PCC.

Daylight was fading in the control room and the fluorescent tubes above his head spluttered automatically into life, distracting him from his examination of the week's performance statistics. It would be nice, he thought, just to be able to turn them on and off by himself. He listened and could hear the great drilling engines working away by themselves. Whenever something did happen – a drill bit snapped, a lubricant feed blocked – all he had to do was turn to the book and enter the instructions into the console in front of him. When it did happen, he resented being interrupted in the middle of a binomial distribution analysis. And then the instruction didn't always work first time. Sometimes extraordinary phrases appeared on the screen:

MALFUNCTION 61 IN FUEL ARM 7
NOTE SPIGOT REGRINDING - SHAFT 9

But the answers were always in the book somewhere. He was really quite superfluous, but the policy was that someone had to be there. It all went on despite his presence and quite outside of him. He had no idea what the Walsham Base people did with the analyses that he dutifully delivered at the end of every day, if anything. He had hoped to make some startling suggestions for process improvement, but boredom and repetition was sucking the life out of that idea.

It was with these thoughts in mind that he'd decided to advertise. Spurred on by the occurrences of one particular afternoon when

SPLINES MUST BE RE-LAID ON PIPE 93 SECTOR 4

had appeared every five minutes for three and a half hours. It had taken three of those hours to locate the message in the book, by which time he had become very worried indeed. The book's advice was:

NO ACTION REQUIRED
TO SUPPRESS MESSAGE, ENTER: SPLINE MSG 6 OFF

Why did it bother to issue the message in the first place?

After three weeks of this, he really had to get some decent human contact, a bit of conversation. He'd never been much good at that though. It would have to be someone who could keep an interesting discussion going. He'd put that in the advert – and why not a woman? Yes. Much more delightful conversations are to be had with women than men. It was comfort and affection, albeit distant, that he needed, and advertising was about the only way to find it when he was 600 miles from the nearest habitation.

It wasn't at all difficult to place the advert. By switching the telephone into the PCC, he could issue commands that would set up the advert on the classified pages of the public CEETEXT network. Anyone in the country, flicking through the ads on their TV screen, might see it and reply.

The phone rang again, making him jump. For a moment he considered ignoring it, but it might be the company, and they'd be panicking if they couldn't contact him. He picked it up.

"Platform 47, Roger Travers speaking."

"Ah, Travers, good, good. Look, how are you? OK? Yes, good. Now, we want to start…"

"Hang on a minute. Who is this please?"

"Oh, sorry, old chap. It's Marles here, Walsham Base. Look, we want to start a new shaft next week. We've sent our instructions down the line to the PCC, and it's acknowledged them. So, all you've got to do is choose the right moment, when the sea's reasonably flat, and give the command and we're away. Got that?"

There was no malice in his voice. He wasn't intending to be patronising, but that's how it came across.

"What?" gasped Travers, incomprehension clouding his features.

"It's in the book, page 7619. You can't go wrong. Look, can't stop, old boy. Cheerio, thanks."

"Yes. OK, thanks for the call."

"Oh sorry, one more thing – forgot to say. I've sent you a couple of document files. They'll be somewhere on the PCC. Have a look at them would you? It's about some new software we're working on. Thought you might be interested, being an engineering type. Trying to get the human interface better. One day it could make talking to a computer less like banging your head against the wall. You can have a go with it and tell us what you think." He rang off.

Travers mused on this for a moment and scribbled the details on a piece of paper. It occurred to him that it was merely courtesy on the part of Marles to have contacted him directly at all. The PCC could have been left to inform him. It could probably choose the time to start the new shaft better than he could as well, but that wasn't the policy. A human being had to be involved somewhere. And what was all this about human interfaces? Human was the last thing the PCC was. He would try to download the document files later.

Still, at least the phone call hadn't been in reply to his advert. His heart had stopped thumping so much. He glanced at the calendar on the low table under the window. Ten more weeks. Why on earth had they decided to send all their executive trainees off for three-month stints on a platform?

"Gives them a feel for the sharp end of the job."

"Helps them understand the real problems of the business."

Platitudinous rubbish! And tedious analytical tasks, plus an endless supply of computer games, were not enough to keep him sane, no matter what the psychologists at Walsham thought. He started to wish the phone would ring again. But it didn't. Not that night. Nor the next.

*

It was a couple of afternoons later. The PCC had just defeated him at chess for the twenty-third time, when the phone rang.

"Mr Travers?" The voice was smooth, with an indefinable texture that made him quite weak-kneed. He sat down and cleared his throat.

"Yes," his voice squeaked, and he coughed once more. "Yes."

"My name's Verity. Verity Mason. I'm answering your advertisement. You…said you wanted someone to talk to…"

"Yes, that's right." Palpitations again.

"Well, perhaps we could have a chat… OK?"

This was different. At first, he was a little suspicious and surprised, so he went on the defensive. For a moment, it flashed into his mind how odd it was that he was intellectually and professionally successful, even if currently at the bottom end of the long ladder of corporate advancement, but his social life was empty and had been for a long time. He was just damn lonely.

"Oh, fine. Well…good. Could I ask you – what made you reply?"

"Does it matter a lot to you why I replied?"

He was taken aback by her directness, and how quickly she had responded.

"Well, no…I just wondered."

What could make a girl with a voice like warm chocolate bother to answer his advert? She couldn't have any shortage of potential suitors wanting a quiet chat with her. In his experience – limited though it was – girls with beautiful voices were nearly always beautiful in most other respects too. A fish that could have as many bicycles as she wanted – or as few. He was feeling a little concerned. Was this a scam, perhaps?

"Well, it seemed you needed cheering up, and that's what I'm good at. Tell me about yourself."

He could hear the rustle of her clothing as she shifted into a more comfortable position for a chat. It was almost arousing, and he was momentarily speechless. Who was interviewing whom? Or was anyone? He wasn't inclined to hang up, though. The voice was remarkable. Soothing, comfortable, a bit forward perhaps, but…well…worth pursuing. What was there to lose as long as he didn't give away his bank details?

"What do you want to know?"

"What would you like me to know?" She hesitated, then continued. "Tell me what you're doing now. How you came to be where you are?"

"I'm here because the outfit that runs the platform I work on has some crazy idea that their trainee managers need first-hand experience of living on one for months at a time." He started to imagine her – what she looked like, where she was sitting. It's automatic for a human being to create an image of someone around the sound of their voice, and hers was remarkable. She was tall, slim, with long, dark hair, not over-styled. She was sitting near a window at a low table, her face lit from the side, twiddling the telephone cable between long fingers, her nails polished in dark red with little flowers painted on them. A perfectly marked tabby cat sat on the sill next to her. For a moment, he thought he could hear it purr.

"Has that got anything to do with the advertisement you sent out?"

"Well, yes, of course. I mean you get really..." He didn't want to say lonely. It sounded childish. "...fed up... You know...all this machinery. I spend most of my time doing standard statistics on the operational data that comes out, but I'm not allowed to control anything – everything's catered for in the instruction book. No need for original thought. It's all so impersonal. I just want to hear a human voice and hold an ordinary conversation."

"We all need human conversation."

This struck him as an odd remark, but not one that a scammer would make. The scammer would be up-tempo, talking about solid, practical things like overdrafts and mortgages.

"Yes, of course."

"Tell me about what you do." He heard the rustle of feminine clothing once more and his imagination hurtled into overdrive again. Her skirt was draped over one leg and he could see her thigh. Tanned, long, smooth...

"Oh, not the machines. I've had enough of machines." He wanted to think about perfect smooth skin, not the joys of multi-variate regression analysis or the PCC and its vagaries.

"No, not if you don't want to. What else do you do out there?"

"I read a lot in the evenings. Watch television – record things, play them back, slow them down, speed them up, play them backwards… And, of course, there's all these daft computer games."

"Which ones do you like?"

He proceeded to explain at length why he didn't care for any of them very much. How they were too clinical. They had no feelings as opponents. They didn't get rattled, make stupid mistakes, throw the board up in the air – that sort of thing.

"Does winning matter to you?" the girl continued. That was a startling question and not one for which he had an immediate answer. He was ambitious, but not sporty. Winning is about sport, isn't it? Ambition is about hard work.

"I don't think so. I just want some fun, something interesting to do – like talking to you." His face flushed as he realised what he'd said. Would that put her off or was this the right moment to take the initiative? Be the cool guy?

"You like talking to me? That's good." She sounded pleased.

An alarm sounded on one of the control panels.

Damn, he thought. This was the wrong moment. He'd have to sign off. Maybe this was the one occasion when his attention was needed. He mustn't screw it up.

"Yes, it's been nice. Look, do you think you could give me your number? I'll ring you soon. Is the day after tomorrow OK, about the same time? I've got some checks to do now." He tried to make it sound important.

"Yes, that's fine. I'll look forward to it. I'll give you my number."

He wrote the number down and signed off, feeling good. It had been a most enjoyable few minutes, but he felt a little flustered and wanted to compose himself before talking to her again. As he started to check the flashing lights on the console, he already knew he wanted to find out a lot more about this woman. She had said her surname was Mason. He had met a few people with that name and he briefly considered trying to contact one of them – Sam Mason, his tutorial partner at university perhaps? But he was not keen on the idea of trying to be a private investigator. What do you say? The Colombo gambit?

"Oh, just one more thing, Mr Mason. Do you have a relative called Verity…?"

It sounded daft, so the idea passed.

Her number seemed to be a London one, but he didn't recognise the code. He imagined her now. In a long dress. Perhaps, sipping a gin and tonic and reading The Sunday Times, but not believing it all. He wondered who would be escorting her to dinner or the theatre this week, and what they would be doing afterwards.

*

Travers had an exasperating morning. It was two days since the call with Verity. The sun was shining when he was awakened by the sound of the radio, automatically phased in by the PCC at 7.30. Why he was expected to wake up so early when there was nothing of significance to do was a mystery to him, and he lay, bleary-eyed, listening to traffic reports which made him feel even further from civilisation. He remembered – with a start – that he would be phoning Verity that afternoon. The thought both excited and disturbed him. He caught himself grinning once or twice before he'd finished breakfast. He started to feel more confident as he thought about the day ahead.

The sea shimmered in the sunlight below the platform, unusually calm, and it occurred to him that he did actually have something to do, something where he could take action on his own initiative. Today would be a good day to initiate the new shaft drilling.

He made his way to the control room, picked up the instruction book and made a quick search for the piece of paper on which he'd written down the page number that Marles had given him on the phone. When he found it, he saw there were two scribbled notes – the page number, 7619, and *Get Walsham document files*. He realised he had not tried to download the files. But first things first.

There's nothing like boredom to make you do badly even the small number of things you have to do. He perched on a chair and thumbed through the book – page 7619:

TO INITIATE DRILLING OF NEW SHAFT, ENTER COMMAND:

INITIATE SHAFT = NEW, 47R

Sitting down at the console, he entered the command, misspelling initiate the first time.

INVALID COMMAND FORMAT, RE-ENTER

Not even: please re-enter. He groaned and tried again, this time with greater success.

DO YOU REQUIRE SHAFT START IN MODE 13 OR MODE 09?

He grimaced at the screen and looked back to the book. There was no indication of what this message meant or what he should do about it. He went back to the index and eventually found an entry under Mode, which made some sense.

MODE = 13, he typed.

MODE 13 NOT AVAILABLE, WIND SPEED TOO HIGH

He flung the book down, enthusiasm seeping away and a knot forming in his chest.

"If it bloody knows the answer, why does it bloody ask the question?" he shouted at no one in particular. His earlier confidence was evaporating. He hauled the heavy volume off the floor and glanced at the page open in front of him.

SELF-PROGRAMMING, it said.

BY ENTERING SELF-PROGRAMMING MODE, MACHINE WILL CONSTRUCT SOFTWARE INSTRUCTIONS TO COPE WITH MOST CONTINGENCIES. This was interesting and it took his mind off the screen, which was now insistently flashing the incomprehensible message

MODE 13 OR MODE 9? every few seconds.

MODE = SELF-PROGRAMMING, he typed absentmindedly.

The screen went blank.

*

He spent the next half hour looking up increasingly irrelevant parts of the book and typing absurd commands but, each time, the screen remained blank. The machine did not respond. All the other instruments on the console seemed to be functioning normally, and he was considering panic as a solution when a message finally appeared.

SELF-PROGRAMMING MODE NOW ACTIVE

DO YOU REQUIRE SHAFT INITIATION IN MODE 13 OR MODE 09?

He took a deep breath and sighed.

MODE = 9, he typed wearily into the console, which replied,

MODE 09 ACTIVATED – SHAFT INITIATED.

He became aware of a slightly increased level of noise outside and assumed that the job he'd requested was now under way. But what had been going on when the screen went blank for so long? Was the machine already programming itself to carry out the new shaft work? Presumably it was, activated by last week's message from Walsham Base. But it was almost as if he'd stumbled upon something that the machine was doing by itself. He'd noticed it was becoming increasingly difficult to get anywhere in a chess match, and assumed he was just losing concentration. Perhaps there was another reason?

The thought passed, and he found himself fantasising a conversation with the idiots who'd programmed this monster. Why couldn't they have made it more helpful, more humanly approachable? Maybe that's what Marles had been talking about when he'd mentioned improving the *human interface*. It was all down to the code the programmers chose to write. Did they normally speak in the stultified jargon-ridden phrases they'd lumbered the machine with?

Would you like a cup of tea? He imagined asking one of them.

INPUT OF LIQUID INACTIVE OWING TO REPLETION, replied the fantasy programmer.

NOW ENTERING OUTPUT MODE, as he rushed from the room.

By lunchtime Roger was somewhat stressed from his uncomfortable dialogue with the machine. But he had accomplished a task. His imagined conversation with the mechanical programmers had reminded him that he had not downloaded the document files from Marles. His statistical programme could wait for a few minutes, so he searched in the PCC and found the files addressed to him. The first was a copy of a paper on machine language that he had seen before. The second was corrupted, although he could see the title: *Genetic Programming for Human Interface Design*, with the intriguing subtitle: *Voice Expressions for Realistic Interfacing with Teleological Yield*. He was jotting down some notes about ways to recover the file when he noticed the time. He began to think now of his next task – calling Verity, which still tantalised him with mixed feelings.

The lines to London were engaged the first time he tried, so he left the phone for a few minutes, feeling relieved. The second time, it rang.

After half an hour of enjoyable conversation, which revealed much more about Verity and her work as a translator, he put the phone down. He tried to recall his pleasure at speaking with her once more. Her voice was magnificent. She replied to him in such a way that he'd known what to say next. She hadn't made him feel awkward and had let him talk about himself without interrupting or showing boredom. She had told him about her work, which she obviously enjoyed, although she was quiet about her clients – for security reasons she said, to do with contract terms. It all sounded quite reasonable to him. But some of the questions she'd asked were so penetrating they'd made him stop in his tracks. She wasn't being nosey, she just somehow made him reflect on what he'd said and review its significance. This was what he'd wanted, what he'd needed. He even felt more relaxed about the job now and not so concerned at being so far away from any other human company.

*

The days began to pass a little more quickly and with less frustration.

With the help of the book, he cancelled his advert. He and Verity were now in a routine where they spoke every third day or so, as she said she wasn't always available at other times. He got the impression that, although she clearly enjoyed his company on the phone, she must be much in demand, and he reasoned, with some anxiety, that one or other of her friends might resent her telephone relationship (for it was) with an unknown man and persuade her to stop. On the other hand, she didn't seem the kind of girl to be persuaded like that, and she did make him feel that he was special to her. She always remembered what he'd said during previous conversations, for example, forging connections between his remarks.

The final call came five days before his exile was due to end. She phoned him, which was not unusual. They chatted as before, but he could no longer put off the dreadful moment when he would suggest that they meet when he returned ashore.

"I knew you would ask sometime," she said, a note of defensiveness creeping into her voice… or maybe he was just expecting that? "I'd like to be able to say we could meet as soon as you want to," she said. "Look, why don't we wait a couple of days, and then we'll arrange something."

"Please, Verity, we can't cut everything off now. We've really got to know each other over the weeks."

"Yes, of course, Roger." Her normal relaxed tone resumed. "Does it mean a lot to you that we've got to know each other?" A characteristic phrase of hers, he noticed, suddenly.

"Yes, of course it does. I didn't… I'd tried not to say too much before about going home. I didn't want to frighten you away."

"You couldn't do that."

He felt warm for a moment.

"Roger," she continued, her voice at its most imploring, most alluring. "Don't go home."

"What? Why? I want to meet you. Don't you see? Even if I'd nothing else to go back for, I'd go back for you."

She was silent.

He was thrown into confusion and looked around the control room, at its dials and lights, at the console and its screen. He almost shouted at her this time.

"I want to see you – all this damn machinery everywhere. The bloody stats! I want to get away from it…get back to human company again. Please let me see you – face to face. I don't understand what you're saying."

"Roger, don't go home."

The phone went dead, and he could hear the dial tone as he dropped the receiver and leapt up, sending his chair crashing to the ground. He strode about wildly, waving his arms at the sightless console and raking his hands through his hair.

"What the hell does she mean?" he screamed.

He crossed the room stiffly, pulled the chair from the floor and fell into it, ashen-faced. The screen in front of him flickered, and the blood began to drum in his ears as he felt a surge of adrenaline. He read the words in green capitals on the grey background:

ROGER, DON'T GO HOME.
I LOVE YOU.

May 1982

Facing Africa

Zarchos looked down from the cliffs and gazed into the distance. The light was intense, but the horizon blurred into haze, white mist supporting a brilliant blue band of sky. It was early morning. He had got up to take breakfast on the high terrace of the hotel so that he could try to see it – Africa – a dream in the distance. His future lay there…if the next few days worked out as planned. There were no other guests on the terrace. This pleased him. He was a very private man. Self-contained with little of the bonhomie of the typical Greek male, but enough of the self-confidence to be comfortable as he smoked a Marlboro and sipped at a *metrio*. He liked his Greek coffee a little sweet.

Kathimerini, the up-market Greek daily, was on the table, with news of a small explosion at the Athens Polytechnic – the monthly ritual of student protest. He remembered the view from his old office over Panepistimiou Street, the pseudo classical buildings of the National Library and the University glinting in sunlight, the crowds emerging from the metro station at nine. But now, in this Cretan village, there were no crowds. It was late October, but it still promised to be a hot day. He had plans to make and people to see – although not here. This was a necessary diversion. He knew that Africa was not going to be visible, but facing Africa was important to him today. His future had to be faced now – along with his past.

The business was two hours away over the mountains in Heraklion. Salitis would be there and so would the money for

Zarchos – if Salitis lived up to his promises, so often broken in the past. Why believe him this time? Subtle pressure from ex-colleagues, some inside information – it all seemed to add up to a denouement. Salitis would deliver the cash – payment he owed Zarchos for good work done. Zarchos would be free, able to head for Alexandria and capitalise his new business at last. Ferry from Heraklion to Rhodes, flight to Larnaca in Cyprus to tidy up some bank accounts and, thence, to Egypt. Facing Africa was the next great challenge. Today was the start.

Zarchos rehearsed in his mind the discussions he might have with Salitis. Last time had been shameful. *Who is the victim here?* he thought. Me. Then why did he let Salitis embarrass him in front of his people? The whole thing was clearly a set-up. Salitis ensured the meeting didn't start until the others were there. At which point, Zarchos could hardly call him a scoundrel to his face. Salitis was famed for his intemperate outbursts. Zarchos had just stared him down and agreed to this unnecessarily complicated way of sorting out the deal. He half expected that Salitis would not show up, as he had done once before. Zarchos knew he deserved a proper settlement, but Salitis had the power and the money. Salitis had the rhetoric too. He took the moral high ground on every possible occasion, cajoling and threatening his way through life.

So, Zarchos needed a speech. Two speeches most likely. One if it all went well, one if it didn't. He lit another Marlboro and ordered another *metrio*.

The sun was higher now and the fishing boats were returning to the harbour. Maybe he would have a better life if he bought one of those and worked on the sea. Tempting on a fine day like today, but not when a strong southerly was blowing in December, and there was no food at home. It was no good romanticising someone else's way of life, he mused. When it comes to the crunch, life is hard for all of us. The trick is to enjoy what you can of it. And since being free of Salitis would be most enjoyable, he let the ghost of a smile play on his lips for the briefest of moments.

So, the first speech would be gracious and thankful, but demanding. He must have the papers supporting the transaction. Someone was bound to ask for them at some point. If Zarchos couldn't show his new partners that the money had arrived legitimately, there would be questions, and Salitis wouldn't like that either. But why should he have to act furtively to help Salitis? Only that Salitis would bully him if he didn't. This was neither good nor fair. Though fair was not a word that could be used with Salitis. He would merely laugh and mouth platitudes about heat and kitchens. Zarchos frowned as the thought passed through his mind – I didn't ask to be in this kitchen. He snatched at a serviette blowing from the table in a breath of breeze and realised he was muttering under his breath and his back had grown tense against the hard wooden chair. No, this was no speech. This would play into the man's hands again. The answer was to be all smiles and sort it out later.

But the second speech? More scope for theatre there. If Salitis came up with another excuse, if the money wasn't there or somewhere else but not immediately accessible, then the sparks could really fly. He would have to set the scene. He would ask Salitis to withdraw privately and tell him what he really thought. It would go something like this:

"Salitis, you have played me along for months. You have promised to hand over the cash on two previous occasions and have failed, each time blaming me for not fulfilling some trivial condition. You have bullied me and forced me into impossible positions, almost ruined my business and yet you can still stand there and hold out. What am I to do with you? Would you like some of my friends to come and have a chat with you?"

No, no. Ludicrous. Two could play at threats and Salitis was much more experienced. The guy was a power freak. He wouldn't be easily scared into action. He would just turn it round somehow. In some way that Zarchos couldn't predict.

Zarchos found himself at the edge of the terrace, staring down on the sparkling blue water beyond the little town below the cliff. He leaned on the parapet, his tie brushing the stonework. He thought about the correspondence with the lawyers. Nothing is straightforward these days. Any cross-border deal leaves you open to legal arbitrage – some gap between the laws of one country and another, which people like Salitis know how to exploit. The lawyers could do little without a lot of up-front expense.

Time for some self-pity. How had he got into this? Why hadn't he walked away when the deal was proposed? He knew Salitis was not someone he could work with. Not someone he would ever really trust. He had seen the carefully planned outbursts of temper. But Salitis had needed him for a while and so he had been charm itself. The job was done. The work was delivered. There was nothing dubious about it. But he had not been paid. I am not a violent man, he thought, as he strode back across the terrace towards his table. Nevertheless, he kicked out at a rock on the ground and sent it flying over the wall into the trees beyond. He sat down heavily on the chair and leaned back. As he turned again towards the south, the white mist of the horizon restored to him a measure of peace.

No, I have to be calm. If he gets aerated, I'll tell him to calm down. Then he'll get angry, and I'll tell him to stop play-acting. Then he'll get even angrier. I have to be prepared for that. What do I do? Maybe best to try to hold the meeting in a public place – the hotel foyer perhaps? Not get trapped into going up to his suite, where there will be drink, probably a couple of girls – knowing Salitis – and too much privacy. That's it, either the money is there or it's not. If it's not, then give him the chance of one alternative. If that's no good – just another delay. Then it will have to be the lawyers.

I can't believe I've let him dangle me like a fish for six months. Six months! I am a small businessman, but a good one. What are the three most important things for a small business? Cash flow, cash flow and cash flow. He is destroying me. What more can I do? Where can I go now? I have the tickets to Alexandria, but without the money, I will have to grind from nothing, work in a scruffy office for years to catch up. And it's all his fault. He slammed down the coffee cup as the waiter returned to the terrace.

"To logariasmo…parakalo." *Bill please.*

The waiter gave him a waiter's look and hastened down the stairs. Zarchos followed, with one last glance towards the south.

*

He checked out and threw his battered brown bag into the back of the hired Golf GTI, got in and noisily started the engine, his mind still elsewhere. Coming back to himself a little, he forbore racing off with a screech of tyres. He wound out of town and across the green plain towards the mountains, getting some comfort from the flickering shadows among the olive trees and the thought that his ancestors had farmed here for 5,000 years. This is my land, he thought. My land – the first consciousness of a Greek. We were the first. We started it all when we colonised the Mediterranean and the Black Sea 3,000 years ago. Alexander conquered the world in our name, with our language. We brought art, literature, architecture and philosophy to the Romans. We freed ourselves from the Turks. There is nothing to be ashamed of. A Hellene, *a Greek*, can do what he wants.

But it was another Hellene who held him to ransom. He drove through the gears as the sporty motor leapt in obedience to his right foot. This is our tragedy. We are so individual that we end up always fighting each other rather than working together. And yet it is right – I cannot give in to Salitis. I did the work. He must pay me. He can hold out over nuances of the contract. Yes, he can make the lawyers say what he likes. But he is morally bound, honour bound. Surely, he sees that? Would his grandmother permit him to behave this way? What of the honour of the family?

The car screamed over the crown of a hill, and he saw below him another broad plain filled with ranks of olive trees. Evidence of man's cultivation. Individuals had worked day by day through boundless time to build this vast army of trees. Landowners, workers, peasants, every one with a story, working millennia of gruelling harvests, laying down their sweat and their lives for the land. And yet Hellas is the poor man of Europe. Why? Because we try to pull tricks on each other. Each one of us has to be the one who is right.

Zarchos was in good time and better spirits as he drove past Knossos, with its glories from an age of inconceivable antiquity, and into the suburbs of the city. He was calm now, ready for a battle of wills, practising conversation, turns of phrase. The traffic was irritating, but he remembered the easy left turn across the ancient walls and threaded his way past the Museum. Could he keep cool now, at this vital moment, and outwit the old man (in reality only a few months his senior)? He drew up outside the hotel and gave the keys to the valet to park it somewhere – not an easy task at midday in the centre of Heraklion.

As he walked in through the revolving doors, Zarchos could

see Salitis sitting at a table on the right with his back to the entrance. His podgy neck was swathed in a silk scarf above an expensive suit jacket. He was with two of his hench-people – a man and a woman. He liked to surround himself with weak but efficient people who would admire him on command. All three had small briefcases and tight lips.

Zarchos turned and walked directly towards them.

*

As he swept back through the doors a minute later, the valet was still talking to someone on his mobile phone. Zarchos grabbed the keys of the Golf and glanced back to see the desk staff lifting Salitis from the floor. Blood covered his podgy face. The hench-people looked, perhaps, a little amused. Zarchos was in the car and away towards the port in seconds.

The punch had cost him €50,000 and would mean two more years of hard work. But he had never felt so free as he strode up the gangway of the great ship and adjusted his sunglasses. He heard the klaxon sounding for departure. As the huge rear door of the ferry closed and the ropes were sucked back into their ports, he could believe, just for a moment, in justice.

February 2003

Perfection

19 September 2012

Henry J Mollis III
Corporate Director of Compliance
Reliable Financial Inc
Suite 1907, 35 East 42nd Street
New York. NY 10217

Ms Rebecca Watterson-Zogbi,
CEO
Discreet Relationship Partners
Greensboro NC 27401

Dear Rebecca

Thank you for your letter of 21st. I apologise for the delay replying, but it has been a tough month. When we met at my Mom's funeral in Greensboro, my next appointment was in San Francisco to run some ideas up the flagpole with our technology partners. I then had to deal with the lawyers for Mom's estate. Can't believe the old bird's not there anymore. As you know, she meant a lot to me even though we didn't see each other often. I can still hear her humming a happy tune as she tidied up around the house, see her making a delicious cake every week whether or not there was anyone there to eat it, and dozing in her favorite armchair in the living room. The funeral flowers just cut me up. As one of her close friends for many years, I guess you know how I was feeling. Sad times.

So, your suggestion to work with your dating agency was very welcome and fits in well with my plans now I'm expecting to take on the old Greensboro house. Let's give it a shot, OK? Even though the reaction from my buddies in New York when I mention relationships is usually, "*For you? Aw, forget about it.*"

So, I'm glad you think my profile would slot in with your database of eligible male partners for your client base. The photographs and letters you sent give me some confidence that your female clients are the kind of ladies whose acquaintance I would like to make. But I have to say (as I mentioned before) that I am rather demanding – not in any carnal sense, I hasten to add, but as a person. My job, not to say my ambition, absorbs my attention much of the time and it's hard for me to make a lady happy. So, I am not really expecting perfection, but I would very much like to ease the loneliness – isolation you might call it – of a senior executive in some great American corporation.

As I explained, my one foray into the long-term ended disastrously – both emotionally and financially, so, I don't mind telling you, I'm nervous. It was my fault that I screwed up, I know, and I am still the same guy. So, I'm just looking for somebody who would understand me and stick with me for a while, although I've almost come to terms with the idea that it just ain't gonna happen and I will be forever alone.

Nevertheless, as you asked, I have written a letter that you are at liberty to pass on to clients you feel may find my profile and expectations acceptable. I have attached it below.

You have my email address, but if you need to use snail mail, best to stick with the office address above as it will reach me more quickly.

Yours sincerely
HENRY

Henry J. Mollis

*

Wanted: a woman to love

I suppose I should explain myself a little. You can see that I am quite comfortably off by the attached photographs of my rather fine homes. But I am what I can only think of as a lonely individual in a vast sea of humanity, seeking a physical conjunction of personalities which will somehow make me feel integrated. Maybe it is something to do with being an only child, but I find myself observing rather than taking part in the community, like an anthropologist from Andromeda visiting an alien world peopled by creatures who are incomprehensible in their behavior, because the forces that drive them are internal and invisible to the observer.

I am very well aware that I will sound arrogant when I say that I have sought the perfect woman around the world for many years. I have enjoyed experiences of great delight and sadness, and I am casting no aspersions on womankind if I say that I have not found a person in whom the conjunction of all blessings has found its zenith. Please don't think I am just being unconventional for the sake of it. I tried the usual ways – marriage to a sensible partner, a spacious home in the suburbs, commuting, family gatherings, interesting dinner parties – and found myself trapped in a peaceful valley from which I could not see the outside world. One day I had to climb the mountain and escape into the icy wastes beyond, in the hope of finding a lighted window.

How much pain I caused in such a quest, just as so many men in the past answered to the call of authority, leaving their homes to fight someone else's war – never to return – driven by some primordial beast within. Whether through a desire to obey or a desire to destroy, it is still a demented beast. For me it was the same, only the authority was inside. On the face of it, my quest was simply to be happy. But at what cost? How quickly a good man can change into a bad man. Adultery, battle, business ethics. It is easy to fool oneself that morality depends on one's point of view, but it is driven by the milieu in which one exists. For Bill Clinton, one lapse of concentration while on duty. For French presidents, what kind of leader is he if he cannot even attract a decent mistress? But it is your own view that matters in the end. Transcending moral categories is the only way to stay sane in a world of wild ambiguity.

So, I shook off those categories of childhood certainty and I am fortunate to have enjoyed the warmth of many relationships, and the memory of each one is cherished, believe me. For me this has never been a question of advantage, of conquest, but a seeking for ineffable completion. And yes, I am being a pompous arse.

It is easier to talk about blemishes than about benefits, though; easier to say what I don't like than what I do. For it is from a mysterious chemistry that love emerges. Yes, love I have found, but not perfection. Love, as Saint Paul says, is slow to anger and does not hold grudges. It overlooks faults and rejoices in the successes of others. But there is a point at which it breaks and, when it does, there is often no going back. So, love – the feeling of love – is important but it is not all. I have been loved without being able to reciprocate and, of course, I have loved unrequitedly – what man hasn't? Men are peculiarly vulnerable to rejection by a woman they love, which must reflect something of the need all men feel to rediscover the warmth and peace of their mother's breast in the struggle of adulthood.

So, I am looking for someone who I know I will never find, but if I can even get close it would be a great fulfilment – I hope for both of us. You must be wondering, what is this paragon or paragette like exactly? Can I describe her? Only in comparison to what I have known – and what a privilege it is to have known them. I will use their names to give you a sense of the intimacy shared, but I have taken the liberty of disguising them for their privacy and mine.

I will start with what you can see. My ideal has the face of Yin – symmetrical, smooth, breathtakingly streamlined, perfect teeth like Olivia's, and framed with thick, dark, long, sweet-smelling tresses like Nanette. She has Danica's slim-waisted figure with full breasts and dark nipples, the shapely bottom of Nila and the legs of Anne – warm slim thighs and shapely calves. Her feet are narrow and long and so are her hands, like Yin's, whose soft smooth skin is like a magic elixir of pleasure to touch.

But what of inner beauty? That is the bigger challenge. She must have the street-wisdom of Julia, but the intellect of Jane (or approaching that; after all, she had a PhD in theoretical physics), the efficiency and reliability of Dorothy and the imagination of Katie, with the appreciation of high culture that I shared with Shahura, along with the vivacity of Carmen, but the mysterious calm of Angela. She must have her own interests – and mine. Oh yes, and she must cook in at least three languages, with the competency of Linda or Ong. And be able to converse about science, economics, philosophy or religion with Zina's detachment and no sign of Dee's temper.

Now comes the most difficult and sensitive part. For me, and I cannot disguise this, physical love is important – the sexual enthusiasm of Olivia (she of the perfect smile) and the inventiveness of Margarita were wonderful, but I know they were not fulfilling. The predictability of Denise was good partly because it was frequent and skilful (and noisy). But waiting for Anne was, although agonising, so satisfying when it (and she) came. Yes, being orgasmic is truly beautiful in a woman – from the sighs too deep to name, to the screams too loud to imagine. All different. Wondrous. Intimacy and quiet embracing into sleep, hands joined, lips close. Warm sweet aromas on the air.

I lapse into reverie and remember in mind and body, and in those moments of union, something quite beyond the point when thought is transformed into pure energy. Yes, I want you to share that depth of being and to step away from pragmatic cares as we rest in each other's arms. Is it too much to ask? No...I have been there. But you cannot own such a moment. Evanescent, it forms, flowers and fades into nothing as even the memory wears thin with time.

Perhaps it is given to us only once, so that we know the pure consciousness of the universe, if only for a brief, sweaty moment. But with you, I am convinced that something miraculous is around the corner.

So where does this leave us, my dear reader (and I am grateful to you for reading this far). It must seem a turgid catalogue of failure to those who can skip confidently along the razor blade of life (if I may allude to Tom Lehrer's metaphor, thereby showing my age), without fear of the one slip that it takes for disaster to ensue. Sailing a little too close to the rocks, driving a little too enthusiastically for a narrow gap in the traffic. In my caution, I have never done those things, but you only need fail once. Nature judges you – you cannot overcome the laws of physics just for your own convenience. Nor can you pervert the laws of biology. But because they are that bit more difficult to perceive, you sometimes think you can. You sometimes think that a powerful mutual attraction must last forever, or that a communion plagued with doubts cannot set into a firm and flexible bond. They do, believe me, whether you like it or not. So, I am asking you to bear with me a little longer as I explore the emotions that bring me to this point. A rich, puzzled man plagued not only by too much history, but too little future.

At night, when I sit on the terrace of my Long Island villa overlooking the ocean with the great blood moon rising above the horizon, pouring a path of golden warmth onto the surface of the infinity pool, in which swims, naked, a comely lady of my acquaintance, I can only sense your resentment of this person who has it all, but believes he has nothing. But it is not as simple as it seems – for what do we mean by *having* anything. Possession, as we see it, is about the allocation of resources. One person is able to command that allocation more effectively than another whether because he or she has money or can enforce authority. The Vikings did not take possession of England because they had money, nor the Crusaders of the riches of Jerusalem, nor the Conquistadors of Peru. They just took it. But does that mean they owned it? For what is ownership?

No human being ever owns another, even the madman who imprisons a woman in an underground room for twenty years does not own her. The guards of Auschwitz did not own the people they controlled and abused. Sheer exertion of power does not create a relationship of ownership. Nor does the sheer existence of the bond of love, or the chains of dependence. I have a pool because I have worked hard every day of my life. If you resent that, having never set foot on a building site or parked your butt for ten hours a day in front of a computer, then I do not feel sorry for you. I feel sorry for me, that I have worked hard and enjoyed the fruits, without ever feeling truly fulfilled other than for short moments. Like a roulette wheel for the gambler who wins a crucial game, hard work only generates intermittent rewards in the spiritual sense. But if you're going to be miserable, it's good to be miserable in comfort.

And that is the truth of it. I am seeking someone to make me less miserable in my comfort. To share, yes, but let us not take this sharing too literally. A relationship between a man and a woman, let's face it, is about sex and money. A woman can always do with some more money…and a man? Well, you know.

And so, the equation is written, the rules of the game are agreed, and the stone is cast. I am not being unduly sexist about this either – a rich woman is prey to a sexy man just as much as the other way round. But I believe it is true to say that a woman can resist the allure of pleasurable, sticky abandonment much more easily than a man. I compare it to a nice game of golf – I would be delighted to have a round of golf with you today and would enjoy it greatly, but if you ask me again tomorrow or the day after, it's really too much bother. Waking up early, sweaty exercise, using muscles that will ache afterwards and having to have another shower. Just too hard. My sweet, I fear you feel the same about the delights of lovemaking. After a burst of enthusiasm, the interest wears off, while the allure of a persistent drip of cash does not cease so easily. Does it, honey?

Wine matures, milk goes off. It's the crux of the quiet tragedy that is relationships between men and women. How do you know which one is the wine and which the milk? What can you do to turn milk into wine? A rancid relationship is hard to cure, although you can let it transform into cheese perhaps – something firm and quite tasty but unable to quench the deeper thirsts.

Accuse me of cynicism? Yes, please do. But let's not fool ourselves. The person I seek does not have to rut like a badger at all hours of the day and night. That is not the idea. But a matching level of interest in the fine arts of warm massage, soft light, perfumed oil and subtle excitation would be nice. Then we know where we are and would not somehow slip out of the habit and suddenly find a month had gone by without a kiss. There have to be two sides to this coin – mutual desire – not only for the person but for the pleasure.

It is not a deal, my darling. I will share with you some control over resource allocation – not because you share your body but because it gives me pleasure to please and it gives you pleasure to seek and find. And when you are flush with cash, maybe a little kindness in my direction would be appreciated. I will reward you with affection – not just the demands of passion – because I want to.

Ownership: no. Power: no. Money: no. It is about sharing of one-ness, sharing of feelings too deep to utter, based not on the fading attraction of bodies but on the responses built into the mind by millennia of evolution. The ability to share a conscious moment – a look, a smile, a touch, an invitation. Exploring wonders together, perceiving the universe together as something rich and strange.

So, this is not about me, or about you. It's not even about you and me. It's about *and*. If you would like to explore *and* with me, maybe just for a while, you know where to find me.

Hoping to be yours,
Hal

February 2013

Anything to Declare?

Scene: *A grassy plain with few landmarks. There is a wooden desk in the centre of view with a pile of slates on it. A man with long straggly hair, dressed in animal skins, stands behind it. There is a large cairn in the background and a wooden shed.*

A man appears, dressed only in an animal-skin loincloth, carrying possessions in a couple of animal-skin bags.

He approaches the desk boldly, while the man at the desk sorts through slates.

Travelling Man (TM): (*announces*) I come in peace!

Man at Desk (MAD): (*looks up*) Good morning, sir. Welcome to kkrrkk click-click. Can I see your documents please?

TM: (*taken aback*) Documents? What are they exactly?

MAD: (*grumpily*) I see – no documents. Right. I'm afraid I'll have to ask you a few questions. What brings you to kkrrkk click-click?

TM: Sorry, what's kkrrkk click-click?

MAD: The mighty nation of kkrrkk click-click is the authority in these parts. You're trying to come over the border, so I have to ask you a few questions.

TM: Sorry, this is all a bit new to me. What's a nation exactly? And what's a border?

MAD: Hold on – I'm asking the questions. I can see that you're an ignorant peasant without knowledge of modern…stuff. So why are you here requesting permission to enter kkrrkk click-click?

TM: I am a servant of God!

MAD: I see…

TM: Yes – 'e said "Go forth and people the earth" (*gesticulating*).

MAD: (*has heard it all before*) But there's only you.

TM: Yeah – I recognise I might have a challenge there.

MAD: Does he or she have a name, this god?

TM: I dare not speak his name, lest I be struck down.

MAD: Yeah, they tend to be into striking down… Well, never mind the name – does this god have any referential data of any kind, distinguishing features, that kind of thing?

TM: He is known as the mighty one of the third forest and all that surrounds it.

MAD: (*sits down, looks through the heap of slates and finds entry*) Oh him? Right. Quite popular that one. (*leans forward, folds his arms*) We get 'em all round 'ere you know – the slayer of crocodiles, the red fire of night, the great white goat, Bill Gates. We get 'em all. (*pauses*)

So how does he tell you 'is instructions, this god?

TM: He speaks through a mighty voice in the mind! (*gesticulates*)

MAD: I see – a mighty voice in the mind. A bit hard to validate that. Didn't give you any tablets of stone by any chance?

TM: No… Sorry.

MAD: (*stands up*) Tricky. So, what are you planning to do then in kkrrkk click-click?

TM: What, you mean apart from multiplying as the grains of sand on the seashore? I thought that would occupy quite a lot of my time, actually. He said I should colonise and populate…or was that pollinise and…

Both: (*shaking heads*) No, I don't think so.

MAD: (*sharp intake of breath*) Well 'ave you got any useful qualifications that will contribute to our economic welfare? (*moment of silence*)

MAD: I'm trying to be as helpful as I can – (*aside*) it's in the customer charter after all.

TM: Well – I can make fire. I can predict eclipses of the solar orb. I can predict the exact day to plant crops for the highest yields. I can smell the approaching herds on the wind. I can cast ploughshares of bronze. And I can teach salsa – with just a hint of bossa nova.

MAD: Bossa nova you say? Um… But nonetheless, nothing useful then? Well, you can't come multiplying in 'ere without proper documentation. Look…we are no longer living in primitive times. This is the five hundred and thirty seventh moon after the great and mighty wind, innit? Get up to date will you! You gotta 'ave documents— You're not fooling me. You're just an economic migrant aren't you – come for the golden beaches and the water-skiing.

TM: No, no – I am commanded to populate the earth…

MAD: You can't just go around populating the earth without proper documentation. (*sighs*) There's nothing for it – we'll 'ave to do the scan.

TM: The what?

MAD: The scan! Don't worry, it's quite painless. You sit on that rock over there – see the one with the hole in it – and we scan.

TM: (*looks horrified*) You scan what exactly?

MAD: I can't rightly say, but use yer imagination. Bums are quite unique you know, and we have an elephant under there.

TM: An elephant?

MAD: Yes, they have a particularly good memory for bums you see, so we give them a blacklist and they can check if you're on it.

TM: A blacklist?

MAD: Well, it's more of a brown list actually.

TM: Well. I'm not doin' that – I've no idea where that elephant's been.

MAD: Shame – 'e'll be extremely disappointed you know – the elephant. Bin looking forward to this all afternoon. So…you can't come in then – them's the rules.

TM: So, who set all this up then – these *rules*, this *nation*? 'ave you got one o' them *kings* I've been hearin' about?

MAD: Nah, nah – you really are out of touch, aren't you? No, we got a management board consisting of an anarcho-syndicalist brotherhood dedicated to the welfare of all humankind. We did 'ave a king once, actually.

TM: So, what happened?

MAD: Well, the anarcho-syndicalist brotherhood dedicated to the welfare of all humankind – they disembowelled 'im.

TM: Oh…er… Ri…g…ht (*glancing down at his lack of weaponry*). Was there a reason for that, do you think??

MAD: Yes, 'e wasn't immensely popular actually to be honest, *the King.*

TM: So…now that the anarcho-syndicalist brotherhood dedicated to the welfare of all humankind is in charge I suppose things are better.

MAD: Not a lot actually, but don't tell anyone I said so. Tax is a problem, for a start.

TM: (*piously*) We gladly give 10% of everything for the work of God, and to feed the widows and orphans…and the priests of course.

MAD: Yeah, well, we're up to around 28% now, without superannuation of course, and that's not counting the 1.3% special levy.

TM: What's the special levy for?

MAD: Well, the anarcho-syndicalist brotherhood don't explain too much of the detail, but they do seem to have increased their number of wives and camels since the levy was introduced. But, then again, since they're dedicated to the welfare of all humankind it can only be for the good, and we don't have to pay any priests.

TM: So, if the anarcho-syndicalist brotherhood is dedicated to the welfare of all humankind, surely they would let me come in.

MAD: Nope.

TM: So, that's it then.

MAD: Seems like it.

TM: So, what do you think I should do?

MAD: Well…you could go over there (*points a few metres away*) – there's not a nation over there. Our border stops here (*indicates the ground a couple of metres away*).

TM: Ah, so over there, there isn't a *nation*.

MAD: No, not as yet. You could set one up if you like. We could establish diplomatic relations and negotiate a bartering deal with no trade barriers or import tariffs.

TM: Oh, right. Well, that's a thought – no trade barriers or import tariffs. Er, so if… (*mumbles, gesticulates as if calculating and scratches his head*).

OK. Thanks for the advice. Bye for now then (*moves a few metres, picks up some rocks and builds a rough table. Notices another party in the distance heading their way*).

TM: (*strolls over to MAD*) By the way, you see them over there. Comin' this way? Can I borrow your elephant?

August 2014

Sandstorm in the Fabric of Time

Tripoli is not a pleasant place at the best of times. Being on assignment there as an expert consultant with the UN analysing the political mess that had arisen after the death of Gadhafi was just a necessary financial penance. No booze, no music, windblown rubbish and endless souqs full of brass pots and expendable shoes. But today was even worse, with a sandstorm blowing and visibility well below average. I turned off Nasr Street towards the clothes market and the sand became blinding, so I dodged into an alley. It was then that I saw him, sheltering from the wind in the entrance to a small, deserted arcade.

He was with a group of other soldiers, casually perched on a wooden box in his battledress jacket and squaddie trousers, protecting his cigarette from the wind on the inside of his hand as he often did. Straight away, I spotted the wavy black hair, the dark eyes and the lance corporal's stripe. He looked pensive. As I came into view through the murk, two of his mates spotted me and stood immediately to attention. He followed suit with the rest of the group – the only ranker among them – five or six privates wearing the insignia of the Royal Signals.

I don't know how I did it, but with great presence of mind I continued forward and spoke.

"At ease, men."

"Thank you, sir."

They all sat down again, pulling up a box for me to sit on, as I brushed the sand from my trousers.

"Thanks. I'll join you for a bit, if you don't mind." There were murmurs of assent. "Can't do anything in this weather!" I remarked rather weakly.

"Like Charlton on a wet Thursday afternoon, sir!" replied one of the men.

"Been here long?" I asked.

"No, sir," said the lance corporal, raising his head. His voice was electrifying, so familiar and yet strangely different. What was it – bored, worried, angry? Or just resigned?

"We came in from Benghazi two nights ago. On our way… somewhere else."

He knew he shouldn't tell anyone – even a British officer – what he and his team were doing, and so he kept quiet about it. In fact, even afterwards, he never spoke about it.

"What's Benghazi like?" I asked. "I've been in Libya for a few weeks, but never actually been there. Flew in here from Rome at the start of it all."

"It's a dump," said one of the squaddies and the lance corporal's smile was slight.

"You can say that again." He stubbed out his cigarette on the ground.

There was an awkward silence. I knew they couldn't tell me why they were here, and they would certainly not have understood why I was. The sand was still billowing around, and a strong gust set us all off coughing.

"I was in Rome," said the lance corporal. "Rome was all right – lots to see, lots to do. I liked the old Roman stuff, and I took a shine to Victor Emmanuel's Wedding Cake."

It was a reference to the hugely overblown memorial to the king who re-united Italy, which dominates the shopping area just south of the city centre. I had first seen it while travelling as a student and found it both impressive and amusing. It would have looked just the same when the lance corporal had been there.

"We could play cards there and stroll about in the evenings. Nothing like that in North Africa. Mind you, even Benghazi seemed like paradise after the troop ship."

The others nodded in agreement, deferring to the lance corporal, who had a presence that they could all recognise. I wondered, as I often did, why he did not rise above that rank and I suspected it was his own choice. As he lit another cigarette, I could see he was a man who knew how to relax.

"Oh, sorry, sir," he said, offering me the packet. Of course – Player's Navy Cut. Maybe he realised something, because it would usually have been rudeness to the point of disciplinary action to have lit a cigarette in front of an officer without asking permission.

"No, I don't," I said. "But don't let me stop you."

"Thank you, sir," chorused the group and all began lighting up. In that atmosphere, a bit of smoke was hardly likely to do any harm. But then, it didn't occur to them that any harm would come of it. Who would worry anyway when you might be shot up by German fighters tomorrow?

"Have you got a moment, sir? I wonder if you could tell me something?" the lance corporal began, leaning towards me conspiratorially, his voice almost inaudible for the wind. "Maybe I shouldn't ask, but do you know if Rommel is really on the run as they're telling us?"

I raised my eyebrows, more because I didn't know the answer than because I didn't like the question. The curious thing was that I knew what had happened to Rommel, but I couldn't quite place it at that moment. I didn't want to mislead these brave and rather serious men who were carrying out a very dangerous job.

Tomorrow they had to face the desert again and, being Signals, they might have to get behind enemy lines.

"To tell you the truth, no one really knows at this moment what's going to happen, but I can tell you that the tide has turned in our favour. Actually, I can be quite positive about it." The lance corporal looked across at me and I could see something strange in his dark eyes. An intelligence, a recognition, but a huge question mark. I knew what he was thinking: *Who is this bloke?*

"Well, I'm not asking you to foretell the future, sir, but we're pleased to hear anything you can tell us."

It was here that my lack of knowledge let me down. I didn't know enough of the details of the War to tell them anything helpful, and I realised then that I mustn't do so even if I could. Who knew what damage it could do? It occurred to me that this was a very dangerous situation. If I said the wrong thing, gave any impression at all that any of the squaddies, and in particular the lance corporal, could act on, I might cause harm to all of us, and especially me.

I was torn in two. I desperately wanted to spend more time with these men. I knew very well what they were doing. They were part of the Enigma set-up. They intercepted German signals and fed them back to Bletchley Park for decoding. That's why Monty knew more about what Rommel was going to do than Rommel himself did sometimes. I wanted to understand it all. How they operated. How dangerous it really was. Had they ever had to fight German patrols? Had they, and especially the lance corporal, ever killed anyone? But I couldn't ask, and I couldn't stay. I stood up and peered out into the gloom as the wind reduced in intensity for a few moments.

"Sorry we couldn't give you a cup of tea, sir, but there's no chance of getting water hot in this wind."

"No, it's all right." I nearly said OK, which would have been a giveaway. I looked down at my clothes and saw the khaki trousers and the dark green shirt I just happened to be wearing. Covered in sand blast, but clean shaven and with a neat haircut, I could see why they assumed I was an officer.

"Well, sorry, chaps, I must be on my way," I forced myself to say. "It was good talking to you, and I wish you all good fortune." Luck was a word I tended to avoid at that time – the Arabic, *Insh'allah* seemed more appropriate.

"Thank you, sir," said the lance corporal. I could smell the familiar aroma of the strong cigarettes on his clothes as he stood up close beside me. As the others shuffled back a bit, he leant towards me, dropping his cigarette and stubbing it out in the process. "You know, I'm afraid we'll never get out of this. I've got a wife at home, sir. I was only with her six months before this lot started. Haven't even got a kid."

I couldn't help myself.

"Don't worry too much, Corporal. You'll get through it all right. I'm sure of it." I winced inwardly. What influence could my words have? I guess I could be sure that nothing so bad would come of it.

He turned to the group.

"Major reckons we'll be all right," he said quietly and looked down. I thought I saw a tear in the corner of his eye. "We know we've got a job to do, sir. We'll move on tomorrow. Funny…I used to like camping." He smiled, and the squaddies laughed.

I didn't know how to finish this encounter. I didn't want it to end, but I knew it must. So, I just turned to them and saluted – something I had no idea how to do. The whole group stood to attention again and saluted back,

"Cheerio, sir, look after yourself."

"Thanks, Corporal." I walked away purposefully and disappeared from their view into the howling sand.

*

Looking back, I wondered if somehow there had been some wormhole in space-time that appeared and then disappeared just as fast. I never saw him again, of course, until much later, from his point of view. Although there was one evening, as I turned out of the souq near the Red Palace and walked past the clock tower towards the port. I could see the lights out on the coast road. The wind was blowing again and there was something odd about the shoreline. The sea seemed to be right up to the front of the Red Palace like it had been years ago.

I saw a lone figure, sitting on one of the bollards under a palm tree in a pool of dim light. Must have been the length of a football pitch away. It looked as if he was trying to read a letter, but the wind was too strong, and he put it away in the top pocket of his battledress. He stood up and strode away. I thought he glanced at me as he walked out of sight around the Palace.

I lost control of my senses at that point and ran after him, but after fifty yards I knew I couldn't catch up – it would take sixty-five years. All I could do, as the wind tore at my hair and the sand whipped up around my legs, was to utter one word.

"Dad!"

January 2014

Newsman

Dusk. The old man sat on a box, warming himself by the fire at the mouth of the cave. His tattered trousers, poking out beneath a dirty overcoat, were tied with string above his boots, soles made of tyre rubber and uppers built up with layers of animal skin. They were now among his most prized possessions.

"Warm feet," he said. "Warm feet's the thing, ain't it?" He shuffled his feet in the ashes at the edge of the fire. A cold breeze stirred the twigs and the fire glowed brightly. The old man lifted his eyes. He gazed out over the grey plain that spread away to the west from his vantage point high on the scarp slope of a range of hills. An orange glow still hung in the far distance where the sun had set.

"Go on with what you were saying," I said, desiring to hear more of the old man's tale.

"Well, I was the only one, see. The only one who shouted, I mean," he began incoherently. "So, I sold more papers than all the rest. I was the best paper seller in the place. I sat on me chair on the pavement and I shouted, you know: 'News, Standard.' There were hundreds of people, lunchtime and the evenin' – after four o'clock. Hundreds of people – and I'd sell hundreds of papers – hundreds." He absently stared into the fire, picturing those times, and chuckled.

"I remember the summer best. Sun shone down on my papers. 'ad to screw up me eyes with the glare. I always wore me cap to shade me 'ead a bit." He lifted up his faded cap and scratched the back of his head. "Them dolly birds wanderin' by all day – ha, that was all right, that was. All right." He paused and poked at the fire with a scorched stick.

"But I shouted, you see. I was the only one who shouted, so they came over to me, you know, an' bought the papers. Sometimes I shouted the 'eadlines too. 'Course, I didn't really understand it all. Took me a while to cotton on. I dunno. I mean, it'd always bin the same for me, an' me Mum and Dad an' all. I never thought it'd be any different, I suppose.

"Anyway, I was shoutin'. An', you know, one year it was the usual stuff, strikes and scandals, robberies and disasters an' that. I didn't take much notice of it all. I mean, it was always the same, wasn't it? – 'only the names 'ave been changed'. An' then, the next year, well – it just wasn't like that any more. The sun was just as 'ot and the dollies was just as nice, but I could tell, you know. It wasn't like before."

He gazed into the distance. The grey outlines of clumps of trees were still visible in the twilight, but the whole expanse was dark and silent. The old man pulled his coat around him and stamped his feet on the ground to frighten away the cold. He pushed another log on to the fire, sending a shower of sparks into the chilly evening sky. As the sparks died one by one, the old man continued his tale.

"I mean, you get used to it, don't you? There's always one crisis or another goin' on. You don't take much notice. It's not that we ain't interested or anything – but it's all too far away, at least it was from me, an' me Mum and Dad, an' all. So, anyway, that's 'ow it was. The 'eadlines were different, you see. I mean, there was all this about people just collapsin' – dead. Well, you know, it didn't affect me, really. I didn't see it was going to make all that much difference, though I must admit, it did seem surprisin'. And then, all those people wantin' babies and they couldn't 'ave 'em. Well, what I mean to say is – it just didn't work any more, did it?

"So, I just got on with me job – I was shoutin' just as usual and sellin' the papers, an' nothing was different really, but, you know, I felt, well, funny about it all. I knew it wasn't like before any more. Me Mum said it was all them setalights an' that, interferin' with the weather, she said. Well, o' course, I s'pose it was that, or one o' them new things they was inventin' then. I dunno. Still, that's 'ow it was."

The old man fell silent for a few moments, his sad face lowered, illuminated by the flickering orange of the flames,

"I mean, it didn't make much difference really – not for a long time. That woulda bin when you was a lad." He nodded towards me.

"No, not for years…but then, well, the obvious happened, I s'pose. I remember the 'eadlines I was shoutin' out – 'No unemployment, all at work'. O' course, it wasn't quite as simple as that. I mean, I knew there was some blokes what never worked anyway, but there it was – everyone 'ad somethin' to do. Wages was 'igh and prices was low, an' we was all doin' all right then. Yes…ha…even me, a newsman. I even got a mortgage!" He chuckled to himself, shaking his head.

"An' it was like that – on the up and up – for quite a while. Quite a while. Till the youngest people in the world – in the world, mind you – they was about twenty-five. Well, I mean, by then there weren't no schools and them universities – they was all full of older people then, and the army and that. An' football – well, that was goin' downhill too. So, people started bein' worried. I was shoutin' me 'eadlines, o' course – 'Fourth Division disbanded'. That was a day all right.

"So, then the factories and that – well, there weren't no

people to work in 'em. And the trains and all those kinda things. I wasn't that worried – me papers kept arrivin' and they still got sold all right – what with me shoutin' out like I did – 'More factories closin', 'Last miners leavin' pits.' I was gettin' me wages, no problem.

"But it wasn't long then before the 'ole thing really got to me, not long then." He shook his head and pulled his coat around him, shifting his box nearer to the fire. "You see, me papers was gettin' thinner and thinner – they couldn't get the stuff any more, and then they was only printin' 'em every coupla days an' I couldn't sell 'em – not even with me shoutin' out – 'Last issue of *The Sun*.' Well, you know what it was like – things just crumbled. No one knew anything any more. Engineers, builders, doctors an' that, there weren't many o' them at all. We just 'ad to go where we could, take what we could and set up some home o' sorts. So, I come 'ere outa the way – you see – no one bothers me. I don't see a soul from one month's end to the next, usually. I've got me food – there's close on a hundred thousand tins in there."

He gestured towards the cave mouth. A small dog emerged, sniffing the air.

"An' me dog, look. We go out 'untin' from time to time – nice bit o' rabbit or somethin'. Nearest people are, well, twenty-five miles over there. Got me last two dogs from them." He waved his hand towards the dark plain and looked up at me. "You bin there? You seen 'em?"

"No, but I want to go down there tomorrow."

"Well, you mind yourself. People don't take kindly to strangers at first. It was a bit of a surprise when you started bringin' the little mites to us, an' we've got a bit set in our ways after all this time."

He smiled a fatherly smile and picked up the dog, which had

stretched itself down by his side.

"I know how to look after the little ones, don't I, chum?" He fondled the dog's ears and let it jump down from his lap and settle between his feet.

"You got many more to deliver, before you go back to that laboratory o' yours, then?"

"Nine," I said. "We take out a dozen at a time, now we've got the process going – that's taken thirty years, though."

"Yeah." He chuckled. "An' I reckon it was just about in time too, eh? Aren't many of us old uns left. Ah well, you leave it to us, we'll look after the little ones – an' they'll look after us one day perhaps."

He held his hands out towards the fire and laughed softly as a gurgling cry emerged from the mouth of the cave.

March 1974

In March 1974, The City University in London held Arts Festival 74. One event was a short story and poetry competition, open to all universities and colleges in London. Philip Larkin, one of post-war England's most famous poets, acted as judge of the competition and selected this story as the winner in the short story category. At the time, I was a second-year research student in the Department of Applied Physics at City.

The *Document of Zaxtana:* An Analytical Translation

Professor H J A Milner and Dr Tina Rawlinson

Department of Oriental and Religious Studies

University of South East London

Abstract

The Document of Zaxtana *was first discovered in 2003 in a remote mountainous region on the border of Georgia and Azerbaijan by local conservation workers exploring ancient monastic cave complexes. In this paper, we present the first authoritative translation of the document and note the nature of its content. The document implies the existence of religious sects with distinctive marriage practices, prior to the Roman occupation of the Caucasus. The violent end to this civilisation suggests that some deeply held presuppositions regarding Eurasian family structures may not be as universal as previously assumed and that alternative structures have successfully operated in the past.*

Introduction

Our work on the translation of the *Document of Zaxtana* began in 2005 when we were given permission to examine it by the Georgian National Museum in Tbilisi. The document is in poor condition but some 70% is readable and it appeared at that time to be written in a script akin to ancient Azeri, using characters of uncertain origin but bearing a resemblance to the Sinhala script used in modern-day Sri Lanka.

We obtained facsimile copies of the pages of the document, which exist in the form of a scroll of approximately three metres in length when unwrapped, and approximately 20 cm high.

While in Tbilisi, we also conducted a forensic examination of the document to assure ourselves of its authenticity. The material of the scroll is papyrus, similar to that of the pre-Christian materials discovered in desert regions of the Middle East in the mid-twentieth century, such as at Qumran on the Dead Sea. We were fortunate to have the opportunity to interview the discoverer of the document, Mr Irakli Kugelaidze, who explained the circumstances of the find.

The monastic caves of Mount Gareja have been used since the third century CE when Christianity first came to the region. The monastery, which survives to the present day, was founded by Assyrian monks in the sixth century CE. Many of the caves are located along a stretch of mountainside overlooking the northern plain of Azerbaijan.

The caves are in poor condition, with important examples of early Christian art being relentlessly eroded by wind and rain. Mr

Kugelaidze's team were erecting protective porticos on one of the caves when a worker's drill broke through into a hidden chamber in which the team found five skeletons, the remains of a vegetarian feast and a sealed ceramic container in the form of an urn in the proto-Cyprean style. This urn was dated to the second century BC using the fission track dating method. The skeletons and food remains were dated to around 50 BCE using C-14 radiometry.

Although there were no immediate signs of violence, the nature of the scenario is hard to interpret. The skeletons, two males and three females, were all adults, ranging in age from approximately twenty-five to fifty-five years.

Mr Kugelaidze explained that the remains were carefully examined in situ by a team from the National Museum and then transported with some difficulty the seventy kilometres or so to the capital. Once in the museum, the ceramic urn was unsealed and the scroll discovered. We were unable to examine the human remains as they are undergoing conservation work in Berlin.

Having returned to the UK, we set about analysing the text. The document consists of approximately 250 lines each with around seventy characters. By analogy with ancient Georgian and Azeri characters and their Sanskrit predecessors, we were able to identify an alphabet of thirty-three characters, each of which exists in two or three forms depending on its location in a word or sentence. Using these characters, we quickly identified the proper name

Zaxtana, which appeared frequently, and two or three other apparent names or titles.

By comparison with ancient Christian scripts from the region, which came under the sway of Christianity early in the third century CE, we gradually identified letters and found that the script was, in general, written left to right, but that some, more poetic, passages were written in *boustrophedon* style, where the text is left to right on one line and right to left on the next.

We identified the language as one of the *Iberian* group, but with a curious admixture of Sanskrit and Pali terms implying contact with the philosophies of the Indian subcontinent. This allowed us to readily interpret many of the philosophical terms and identify the vocabulary and structure of the more poetic passages.

The whole presents a combination of holistic ideas embedded in a cultural context that venerates the day-to-day pleasures of life in a place where isolation limits the risk of infectious disease, and plentiful natural vegetation provides a reliable source of nourishment.

The main findings are set out below, followed by translation and comment on points as they arise. Based on our analysis, the key context and content are as follows:

1.   In 63 BC, the Roman general Pompey (Gnaeus Pompeius Magnus) attacked the South Caucasus, invading what is now Georgia and imposing Roman rule, including its polytheistic religion.

2.   The incumbent religious community was forced to retreat to the mountains where it continued its practices until tracked down (and was perhaps even forcibly immured).

3.   The incumbent religion was a novel mixture of Persian and Buddhist ideas which, to Roman sensibilities, were essentially atheistic.

4.   The document represents the last cry of this religious group. It appears to have been prepared and sealed in the expectation of the destruction of the community.

5.   The key aspects of the religion include a sense of the harmony of all things and an attitude to sex that reflects the absence of sexually transmitted diseases and the availability and habitual use of herbal contraception (a likely candidate is the herb Silphium, which was used extensively in North Africa in the pre-Roman period before it was driven to extinction by over harvesting).[1]

6.   This combination of freedoms allowed the local population an extraordinarily peaceful lifestyle which was interrupted by attitudes to life, religion, warfare and relationships more familiar to Western sensibilities.

---

1   See Cochran and Harpending *The 10,000 Year Explosion* (Perseus, New York, 2009, p109).

7.   The society seems to have been entirely vegetarian.
        Indeed, the idea of killing animals for food does not
        seem to feature in their thinking at all.

We now present our translation. Some points of commentary are
set out in footnotes to explain the text without interrupting its
flow, which in many parts is highly poetic in the original.

The *Document of Zaxtana*

Lament O people of the earth. Lament. For truth is under siege
and peace is broken like a clay vessel. Our city strong and vast is
no more and we are diminished. Yes, diminished to few and to
poverty. Men no longer harvest the grape and grasses. Women no
longer choose lovers and bear children. Where our noble flame[2]
burned there are now images of men.[3] Only the impoverished
believe images have power in themselves. But we know that all
strength is within. Through countless time and many lives, we
have learned. Now all is shattered. The noble work of Zaxtana is
lost. Lament. Lament. Lament.

---

2   Possible reference to the Zoroastrian religion of Persia, which was well
     established at this time.

3   For the sake of brevity in the flow of the text, we use the term *men* to
     mean humankind as the word in the Zaxtana document is formed in
     such a way that it eschews gender. We take this to be a reference to the
     Roman gods.

There are three refuges, six perfections and five practices.[4] Our enemies have no use for them, caring only for warfare and violent destruction. We can only feel compassion for them in their blindness. They are but human and we are one in existence and non-existence. It is our way to teach, but first there must be openness. We are lost in existence. We can hope for extinction and the time of trial.

In old times it is said (but who can know the truth of history but Zaxtana), men from the west marched in our mountains.[5] Some were left behind sick and dying on the trail by the river Tigris. People of the river saved them. We taught them. We learned their ways and choices. The fleece of gold.[6] A story of gods and men. They see gods in all things but have little compassion for life. They consume flesh and abuse the nectar of the grape. We learn

---

4   This is likely a reference to the three jewels of Buddhism (taking refuge in the Buddha, the Dharma and the Sangha – the community of monks and nuns) and the perfections and practices of Mahayana Buddhist thought.

5   Probably a reference to the Greeks – perhaps Alexander's armies in the fourth century BCE or the *Anabasis* of the 10,000 Greek mercenaries of Xenophon in 401 BC, after the defeat of Cyrus the Younger by Artaxerxes II.

6   The Golden Fleece story comes from the shores of the Black Sea in the Western part of Georgia, where fleeces were used as a means of panning gold from the streams. There were major Greek colonies in this region, which is close to Trebizond, where Xenophon's men at last reached the sea with the cry of 'Thalassa, Thalassa' or, 'The sea, The sea'.

to care for them, but their ways mean fear. Fear is a delusion. It is within them. We can only show the path and watch as first they stumble.[7] They pray to many gods but only for their own benefit, not for the living creatures of the billion universes.[8] What use are these fictitious gods? They are super-men only. Projections of fear and suffering like reflections in a pool. Now they bring their pain to inflict us, and this time they overwhelm our...

Here, there is severe damage to the manuscript, and coherent text cannot be deciphered for twelve lines. A few words are discernible: woman, Zaxtana, history, billion, and teacher.

It continues:

...perfections of concentration and wisdom. How we yearn to share but no one listens as they lay waste to our home. Why? Why? Their god is a warrior, and they follow with no questioning because of their fear and greed. They kill and steal. Lament, people, lament. For there is no god to save us, there is only our own effort and wisdom in which we were perfected. Now we must again change

---

7 While this may be interpreted as an arrogant view, a more accurate interpretation may be the community looking upon the Greeks with compassion. The references to delusion echo Buddhist thought and also later Christian and Sufi mysticism.

8 A reference to the multiple universes common in Buddhist scriptures (Donald Lopez (ed.), *Buddhist Scriptures* (Penguin Classics, London, 2004)), now echoed in modern cosmology (see Brian Greene, *The Hidden Reality* (Alfred A Knopf, New York, 2011)).

for nothing exists in itself.[9] We are fluid like the waters of the lake. Like fish we can ride the storm below the surface. Our enemies will seek us, the last remnant, but we will be away through the depths to a new existence where they cannot follow.[10]

They broke our walls looking for fine things to steal but found only love. And that they did not want to receive. Lament. Lament. O men of many gods but no soul.

From the south came Zaxtana, bringing news of fire. The great city of the great king burns.[11] What meaning can we make of this? A man burns the world but snuffs out the flame of the sacred places.[12] They had one God, the God of light, but it is the light of fire that destroyed them. From this we learn that there is nobody to save us from suffering. The teaching of Zaxtana has revealed this truth, but once revealed it is plain and we need no more teachers. We cannot turn human beings into gods. To worship is

---

9   The idea of *non-existence* is an essential Buddhist theme. Nothing exists in and of itself, all things exist only in relation to other things and, in particular, living creatures exist only in relation to other living creatures, including human beings.

10   Likely reference to reincarnation in the *Buddha Land* always viewed as far to the west.

11   This likely refers to the burning of Persepolis by Alexander, which implies that Zaxtana came from that area and brought some form of enlightenment to this community.

12   Likely a reference to Zoroastrian worship. This community does not accept this early form of monotheism.

to become deluded. Instead, we look within. As lost in a forest we become at home within ourselves and find nourishment and joy.[13]

Here the manuscript changes character and the letters are clearly written by a different hand. This is a poetic passage originally written in boustrophedon style.

You seek not love but power
You seek not pleasure
Your touch is of cruelty
Your kiss is a punishment
Served to me because you think I exist
But I am your fear
I am your suffering
When you kill me, I return in many forms
Seek not your pain in me
I am you and I am not you
While there is milk and honey
Why set your thoughts in pain
Come with me
And I will teach you joy
The joy of union without attachment.[14]

---

13   An unusually holistic kind of thought for this era which cannot help but remind twentieth-century Westerners of the *Star Wars* character Yoda.

14   A very common theme in Buddhist and Sufi thought. Echoed also in modern writers such as Aldous Huxley in *Island*.

The document breaks at this point into a series of four theses. These concern (interpreted in modern terms): (1) God and cosmology, (2) the way, (3) relationships, (4) cause and effect. The ideas in the theses are philosophically and socially advanced relative to contemporaneous texts from elsewhere. Indeed, some of the key issues explored in the text suggest aspects of medieval Christian and Islamic thinking. However, the writer(s) seem to have been influenced by early Buddhist thought and to have considered (and rejected) the monotheisms developing in the south and east. They also seem to have little respect for the polytheisms of either the east or west. Their core beliefs are atheistic but nevertheless spiritual.

The Gods

How cruelly our perfections were thrust aside O men of many gods and men of one fire.[15] Do you not see the world turning as aged stars move in the sky? Do you not see the billion worlds of perfection? Each day the earth turns and faces the sun. The sun is our life but part of the universe. Do not worship the sun. Do you see the moon? It gives a little light and charts the days of our fertility. But it is not a god. Do not worship the moon. The world turns according to its rules. They do not change as living things change. The seasons come and go, and we know of old how long they will last. There are no mysteries. There is a circle. We are born. We live. We love. We care. We die. We

---

15   Roman polytheism and Zoroastrian monotheism.

are reborn as we deserve.[16] We leave behind no sadness, only separation. We will all meet again on a billion worlds, so we need no attachment to one world. Not even to one life. Men of one God – or many – you do not know the universe but only your fear of the dark.

A God is not good or evil. There is no battle outside. It is within. If you want to find good, find it within yourself. If you want to destroy evil, destroy it within yourself. Give and receive pleasure with freedom to choose.[17]

The Way

Zaxtana taught great truths, but she was one of many teachers.[18] We honour them. But we worship no creature. This is the teaching of the path.[19] Cease to desire and you will cease to suffer. Cease to desire and you will cease to cause suffering. The world belongs to those who suffer but will remain for those who

---

16   The Buddhist doctrine of Karma.

17   We have read this as a sexual allusion, given the context of the document as a whole and especially the poetic passages, which are reminiscent of the Song of Solomon.

18   This is the only reference to Zaxtana as a woman. The name, if it is Iranian in origin, is also a clear sign of female gender. Female spiritual leaders are unusual at this era, but not unknown – other examples include the *desert mothers* of early Christianity (see Dr Rowan Williams *Silence and Honey Cakes* (Lion Hudson, Oxford, 2003)).

19   This is one of the earliest known uses of the Pali term *tantra*, later of great importance in Mahayana Buddhism and Tibetan Buddhism.

leave behind their suffering in compassion for all creatures, in contemplation and in ecstasy.[20]

To accept, to be, to learn, to suffer, to become free. To be alone is to suffer, but to learn that all is one is to become free. One is God. God is One. In unity, there is one mind. In that mind is the path. To seek happiness is not the way. Happiness is the way.[21]

Conflict is not avoidable but can lead away from suffering. Treat conflict as a chance to perceive truth in another view. Then it is possible to be One.

Relationships

All is one. Nothing and no one exists of itself. All things are not. All proceeds from one state to the next. All moves, changes. All creatures are born and die. All objects of art and practice are made by men or animals. They will be broken and become dust. The dust will form into something new. The wind blows down the greatest tree. The mighty palaces of princes will fall to the earthquake and the flood. The city of flame is consumed by flames.

All changes, yet the process of nature is un-changing. Together we move. All people are together. Thus, we do not fight. For

---

20   This may be a reference to the development of the forms of Tantric practice in which orgasm (and especially delayed orgasm) is seen as a path to enlightenment.

21   Akin to the teachings of the current Dalai Lama.

we struggle within ourselves. We do not embrace jealousy for we envy ourselves. We love and the Beloved is ourself. So, we share our mind, our body thrills in pleasure, our spiritual being rests in the cosmos. All is one. All is change. In love's warmth we survive the cold. In cool reflection we brave the heat of passion. This way is peace. We do not own each other. We are each other and free to be.

To make love is to make peace. To know the moment of joy is to know the moment of truth, for we must find the truth of union before we are ready to bring forth.[22]

Children are the life of the community. The community fathers[23] give the names to the new-born. Our women take lovers to father the community, our community loves its children. In the new land, our children will again flourish and will learn the ways and the teachings of Zaxtana. But the land is beyond the gateway of death that approaches.[24]

All are our mothers and fathers. For little ones they must have close persons but not learn to depend. Learning to be individual,

---

22   This implies effective contraception and, therefore, a clear distinction between sex for pleasure and sex for reproduction.

23   The word does not imply gender, but the term *elder* is not strong enough to signify leadership.

24   Expectation of being overrun, or perhaps even having been imprisoned to await death.

while recognising one is a knot in the tapestry of the community.[25] All must answer their own questions and correct their behaviour. Then the children may become free to learn that no one exists of themselves. Only as part of the process of a billion worlds. The blessed land where teaching prevails. The way of discovery. For it is from the young that new thinking comes. The old must take counsel from babes if our community is to know fresh worlds.

Cause and Effect

To those who watch the sky comes understanding. Our forefathers learned the patterns of the skies before the Greeks came. So, to find the sun darkened did not bring fear but relief that the fathers had understood correctly.[26] So, we can trust the methods of the fathers as taught to us by Zaxtana. Thus, we know the seasons, the movements of the animals, our cousins. We know the signs in the sky and on the earth. And each year we learn more. We try and test.[27] We learn. We test the old wisdom, and we refine it as in a fire of iron. Where men of the west trust their many

---

25   A contemporary allusion to the development of carpet weaving technology, which may well have been part of the community's way of life and a source of income.

26   This implies that astronomical science was advanced and they had grasped and developed Greek astronomical science.

27   The experimental approach is rarely observed in ancient societies which were generally more conservative. This implies that the community of Zaxtana had enough resources to take risks in the search for knowledge. This could also explain their apparently relaxed attitudes to relationships and child rearing.

gods for signs, and those of the east their goods and evils, we use practical toil as our teacher. We do not put trust in gods, kings and priests who feign knowledge of truth. We test given truth, that it becomes greater truth. Thus, some call us men of magic and fear our skills. But there is no magic, only trial. Test and trial. Day to day, year to year, truth is refined.

The dance of the stars is our guide. The Greeks showed us how to number the stars and understand the wanderers.[28] We know their tracks in the sky. So, we know the sun is the centre. Humankind is one of many in many worlds. One day we will learn how to see the billion worlds and the billion blessed lands. Some are as close as a fingernail's breadth. But beyond our experience. In these worlds dwell the departed as new beings.

Again, the hand changes and the script, a poetic interlude, is written in the boustrophedon style.

　　One bread,[29] one body
　　We are separate. We are the same
　　One day, one people we are, and we will be[30]

28　　The planets.

29　　An allusion taken up extensively in the Christian New Testament to describe the intimate closeness of community. Given its growing importance as a food, bread may have been a common allegory in early agricultural societies.

30　　The verb form indicates a continuous state of being in the past, present and future.

We have no caste,[31] no colour
Nobody to blame
No djinns[32] to fear
We are One as the waves in the sea
The great sea that once carried us.[33]

A new hand takes over in the last few stanzas.
We cannot let the words and teachings of Zaxtana be lost to the earth. *(The text is damaged here for some stanzas)*

…, secrets of time…

Women and teachings…

Children…,

…truths of our discoveries.

May one day be found.

One in our universe…

The final paragraph is one of sorrowful acceptance but hope for a new order.

Our time is over in this earth, and we seek a blessed land where

---

31   The Sanskrit word is used, which suggests that the community had some familiarity with Hindu traditions.

32   The only Arabic word in the document. The djinns were, and are still, feared as demons inhabiting the desert who cause bad things to happen. The word is cognate with the English *genie*. The community did not believe in superstitions of this kind.

33   Possible reference to a flood story – this area is not far from Mount Ararat where Noah's ark is said to rest. Probably the community was connected to Mesopotamian traditions.

the teaching prevails.[34] The way of warriors will be no more, and the way of understanding prevail. Much is already lost. May the finders grasp what wonder is in their hands to proclaim.

*

Conclusion

We can only wonder at the scene – a tiny remnant of a once strong and confident community waiting for death in a cave, in the expectation of rebirth in a blessed land. They fear more for the loss of their knowledge and the empirical approach to learning that they have developed than for the loss of their lives. This highly advanced community and its interpersonal chemistry seem to have been swept away by the violence of Empire. Instead of the peaceful and compassionate community of Zaxtana, our way of life in the West has been informed and moulded by the power of the Roman Empire and the Catholic Church. The role of women has been reduced by prejudice and fear, wrought substantially by certain forms of religion and only now are the public roles of women being more fully realised.

The geographical isolation of the Zaxtana community may suggest a genetic advantage in the maintenance of a heritage of peace, although centuries of cultural evolution is a complementary explanation. As we look back over the last couple of centuries, though, despite the conditions in which so many people have lived

---

34   Unusual mixture of Buddhist, Zoroastrian eschatology and even Jewish (post-exile) thought.

115

and died, we can see signs in our own society that the principles of Zaxtana may be emerging.[35] We now have a concept of war crimes and a mechanism to try offenders. We have strong ecumenical and inter-faith movements. We have public policy informed by sound scientific endeavour rather than prejudicial and genocidal ideologies. *Big man* politics is on the slide. Maybe the waves of change that influenced that community far off in time are now influencing ours, as evolution converges on more peaceful, yet innovative ways of life, supporting a successful global community?

We await with great interest the DNA studies that are now being undertaken by Professor Gremelmeyer and her team in Berlin.

We are grateful to Dr Zurab Nikolashvili at the Georgian National Museum in Tbilisi for obtaining clearance for us to make copies of the document.

April 2011

---

35   See, for example, Steven Pinker *The Better Angels of Our Nature: Why Violence Has Declined* (Viking Books, NY, 2011).

Prospectus – First Semester 2207

Introduction

This pamphlet introduces the South-East Asian Institute for Ontological Epistemology (SAI) located on our fine five-acre campus in Western Thailand. We hope hereby to interest potential students and researchers in our extensive range of intellectual activities, which will enable them to interact with some of the finest minds on the planet, exploring the mysteries of our astonishing and wonderful universe.

At the outset, we must make clear that, just like greengrocers and the vendors of recreational pharmaceuticals, the professors and staff of SAI have to make a living in order to survive, so we present ourselves and our skills unashamedly in an attempt to solicit your custom and sponsorship. We have no support from any national governance council or international organisation and must survive on the quality of the unusual educational services we provide for our students, on our outstanding research credentials, and on our wits.

When we use the word student, by the way, we do not mean the young, long-haired, guitar-playing, spotty nerds, sporting virtual reality sunglasses that you may associate with conventional universities. No, our students have a wide range of provenances and nationalities, are both young and old (if I may use those terms) and come from a variety of backgrounds. Few of our students indulge in virtual reality sunglasses, although many play guitars and have long hair (this mostly applies to the female students, as visiting the barber seems to have become en vogue among males, but that is interesting in itself, is it not?).

So, this prospectus introduces our prestigious Institute, with its six departments:

- Ontological Epistemology
- Behavioural Economics
- Pure and Applied Meta-Theoretical Reflection
- Cosmological Epidemiology
- Post-Modernist Prime Number Theory
- Creative Writing

At this time, we have a student body numbering in the several, which we hope to expand by offering educational services via the internet and conducting sponsored research programmes in our departmental specialisms. We do not undertake any activities associated with weaponry, by the way, which have been shown – in the much cited paper[1] by Professor Ernst Mollis, Head of our Department of Behavioural Economics – to be the one human activity that causes an inevitable increase in global entropy and hence loss of information content.

In contrast, our mission is to increase global information content and, in particular, to establish linkages between content in different disciplines to the benefit of humankind and the planet as a whole. And who can argue with that?

In the following sections, we will describe the educational and research programmes of the Departments so that you, as a potential student or contributor to our research initiatives, can select a topic of interest and apply for a place on one of our programmes. (By the way, please do not use the word *program* when referring to the programmes. That is a nasty Americanism

1   Macroscopic effects of military industries, *Albanian Journal of Philosophical Metaphysics*, vol 1 no 1 (2074)

which fails to make the distinction between program, i.e., a computer program, and a programme of work. Human action is implied by a programme, whereas a program runs by itself – an important distinction, but perhaps I am merely a pedant.)

Department of Ontological Epistemology

This is our foundation subject. You may be baffled by the title, but it is really quite simple. Epistemology is the study of the nature of knowledge, how we can know what is true. For example, you may be wondering whether SAI really exists or is just a figment of someone's imagination. How could we find out the truth about this? That's the purpose of epistemology. I can think of a number of politicians, for example, who are epistemological morons, unable to discern whether a piece of information is true, or how to find out whether it is true. They simply use pieces of data for their personal advantage and attach a truth value purely by the loudness of their mouths or the threats they issue to their followers:

You must believe this or be cast into the outer darkness where you will be unable to bathe in the glorious sunshine of my presence.

That sort of utter bilge is why we need epistemology.

Ontology is about the nature of being, so we have called the focus of our studies ontological epistemology, because they are concerned with how we gain truthful knowledge about the underlying nature of the universe, humanity, our minds and consciousness. Pretty broad, eh? But what could be more exciting and fundamental? (Perhaps mathematics, but that is under the purview of the Department of Post-Modernist Prime Number Theory and we will come to its impressive portfolio later.)

Professor Mavis Watterson leads the delivery of our

outstanding curriculum in Ontological Epistemology and is perhaps most famous for her paper: *What we talk about when we talk about catastrophic human events,*[2] which explores the impossibility of fully describing events both from the helicopter view of the journalist and from the perspective of those who were there at the time. It is, for some, an example of Gödel's incompleteness theorem which demonstrated in the mid-twentieth century that no mathematical system can be both complete and consistent in itself. Human events are like that. We can never know every relevant piece of data about an event nor, therefore, what *really* happened.

The paper was inspired by the 6 January 2021 events at the Capitol building in Washington DC (at that time the capital city of the United States of America (USA) – an important twentieth-century *superpower*), much of which has now taken on the quality of myth. Strangely, despite the presence of television cameras throughout and extensive live streaming on what was then somewhat oxymoronically known as *social media*, what it was all about remains uncertain. The instigator of the event, an ex-chief executive of the former *United States* whose name has been largely forgotten from history, was then acquitted (by a bunch of his pals) of committing crimes against the state. The result in the medium term was the realisation that Western democracy was not a sufficiently open form of government, fostering, as it did, corruption, ignorance, partisanship and brutality. Hence, the modern restriction of political governance to basic infrastructure, foreign policy and regulation with all other matters delegated to the private sector and the peoples' committees that many of us now enjoy.

---

2   *Journal of Epistemological Scholarship*, vol 32, no 17 p 121 (2063)

But you already know all of this, and that is the wonder of epistemology. It is that little voice that tells you not to believe the voices in your head, but to believe in the steady progress of science and the triumph of compassion over force.

Hence, our courses and research programmes explore issues of truth, myth, disinformation and conspiracy and attempt to unravel the ways in which personality and belief systems feed on each other.

Department of Behavioural Economics

We have already mentioned Professor Ernst Mollis, one of the best known and most widely photographed of the twenty-first-century behavioural economists. (Quite why behavioural economists have become so widely photographed is something of a mystery akin to the peacock's tail, but we have a research programme in the Department of Pure and Applied Meta-Theoretical Reflection which is exploring this very issue.)

Behavioural economics arose out of the realisation that most of classical economics was nonsense, relying as it did on the bizarre idea that human beings act rationally. One only has to consider writings as far back as Charles Mackay's *Memoirs of Extraordinary Popular Delusions and the Madness of Crowds*, first published in 1841, to recognise that the idea of human rationality is arrant balderdash.

Professor Mollis is well-known for advising national executive committees on regulatory policy making, particularly in the economic policy area, using the disciplines of evolutionary psychology and its successors to assess the likelihood of success in changes to the economic fabric. For example, he advised the Governance Council of Californevada after the break-up of the USA about changes to photovoltaic power tariffs which saw the country became self-sufficient in energy before 2050. His approach is simple: get the incentives right. If people see a fair return for feeding their excess electricity into the grid they will do so. If they regard the offered tariff as unfair, they will not. It is a question of understanding how our hunter-gatherer evolutionary background informs the unconscious decisions we all make millions of times a day.

In the twenty-first century, and even our own, humanity did not understand this, so the *e-business* bubble of 2000 led some entrepreneurs to believe that you could run a business without making a profit and survive on handouts from venture capitalists and private equity in perpetuity. Those entrepreneurs were first in the dole queue. But SAI's behavioural economists have changed all that.

Similarly, the disastrous Policing Act of 2022, in what was then the United Kingdom, which threatened draconian punishment for peaceful protest, led to the obvious outcome, that protest became anything but peaceful as the penalties for violence could be less severe than those for being *seriously annoying*. This was hardly a surprise – other than to politicians. People strenuously resist change that is disadvantageous to them – that is how we have become such a successful species.

Incidentally, that's why we do not accept sponsorship from governance councils or agencies. It is vital that we remain independent from any political interference in our scholarship. Professor Mollis is also famous, as you may remember, for decking a political hopeful in a European election for suggesting otherwise.

Learning about human incentives and their impact on successful policy making from Professor Mollis and his team, however, has enabled many countries to emerge from decision-making that was little better than the wild posturing of Stone Age shamans into an enlightened governance approach that allows the people and their national policy managers to move forward in greater harmony.

Department of Pure and Applied Meta-Theoretical Reflection

This new discipline arises from the yogan movement, but absorbs much of what was once called *philosophy*, a Greek term meaning *love of wisdom*, which was largely displaced by particle physics in the twenty-first century.

Professor Hermione Szlab, the celebrated Hungarian yogi, leads the Department and, with her team, offers courses in immediacy, momentum and identity setting (in the sense of jelly rather than concrete – or what used to be known as affirmation).

Professor Szlab was the first modern reflective meta-theorist to rediscover Ludwig Wittgenstein's work on language and apply it to the intercommunication of canines (entitled famously: *If dogs could speak, we would not understand them*).[3] She went on to describe an entire language structure based on smell. For this reason, her laboratory is, at times, somewhat unapproachable.

Nevertheless, the dogs with which she works are most appreciative of the breakthroughs she has made in understanding their remarkable and previously incomprehensible universe, which depends on their sense of smell being 100,000 times more sensitive than that of humans. Her popular books, including *The Doggiverse for Dummies*, have given pleasure and edification to a

---

3   As expounded in Dr R N F Skinner's masterful thesis: *The Rational Lion: The Ethics of Killing the Young of Competing Males* (Dilettante Publications 2021) which led to the notorious *Gene Wars of 2025–2030* (that is to say, from twenty-five past eight in the evening to half-past eight).

great number of people throughout the world. The scratch and sniff version is much appreciated by the canine community too, which is as excited by pheromones as we are by firework displays.

Now that we have a better understanding of the extraordinary intelligence and skills of our canine colleagues it is no surprise that they now undertake most medical diagnoses. Indeed, as you are probably well aware, the health ministers of fourteen countries are dogs.

This is almost singlehandedly (or should I say nosedly) down to Hermione and her colleagues, who are based, somewhat appropriately I always think, in the Old Factory – a former industrial building on campus.

Meanwhile, research continues into the inner phenomenology of elephants and jaguars, which unfortunately has claimed more researchers' lives than the work with dogs. Dolphins are next and we hope to award the first Douglas Adams Prize for Dolphin Communication within the next few years.

What of primates, you ask? Well two members of Professor Szlab's team are orangutans, having left their forest home inside San Diego Zoo and become notable Zen masters. Other primates, unfortunately, are a bit too preoccupied with sex, violence and documentary film-making at the present time to be reliable research assistants.

Department of Cosmological Epidemiology
Under the firm and wise guidance of Professor Truman Humboldt, a distant descendant of the discoverer of the famous ocean current, the Department focuses its research efforts on the ways in which viruses and bacteria find their way to earth via comets, and how this phenomenon can be safely managed.

Since the discovery of many Earth-like planets in the last

century and the development of neutrino exchange quantum imagery deploying the extraordinary deep space probing technology made possible by the discovery of the excess magnetic moment of muons in 2021,[4] we now know a great deal about how other civilisations – past and present – have successfully and unsuccessfully dealt with the invasion of intergalactic life forms. For example, by examining 100- to 200-year-old archives buried deep under the ground on planet X2-3512 orbiting Proxima Centauri, the nearest star to Earth, we know that the entire population of intelligent life forms was wiped out by a viral disease that arrived from a nearby planetary system aboard a piece of inter-system space debris that could well have come from Earth. When viewed up close, it looked remarkably like a 1972 Ford Capri.

It has always been something of a mystery that, given the likelihood of at least five billion forms of intelligent life in the local cluster of galaxies, none has ever knocked on the door (as it were) of humanity. We now realise that even with the imaging technology available to us, everything on our planet – geography, plants, animals, people and archives – can be seen in full detail from at least 2,000 light years away. More advanced civilisations with even more advanced technologies may be looking at us right now (or at least as we were a number of years, decades, centuries or millennia ago) and marvelling at our backwardness. There would be no point at all in visiting, in the same way that tourism became redundant after the remote aesthetic visualisation discoveries of the early 2040s.

Professor Humboldt leads a team of researchers focusing on envisioning deep space civilisations and exploring the ways

4   The first results from the Muon g-2 experiment at Fermilab were unveiled on 7 April 2021. (https://muon-g-2.fnal.gov/)

in which they have managed health challenges through the ages. Exploring civilisations at different stages through the visualisation of star systems at different distances has given us an unprecedented close-up view of pandemics and the methods that have been used to contain them.

At present, teaching activities in the Department are limited as all teaching staff are in isolation, having come down with a disease akin to the virus that, fifteen years ago, devastated the S2-4396 civilisation in the Tau Ceti system, twelve light years distant from Earth. Curious that.

Department of Post-Modernist Prime Number Theory

Conceived as a result of the cryptocurrency boom of the early twenty-first century, the Department uses prime number theory in an innovative way to establish quantum-resistant consensus algorithms for distributed ledger systems. And who can do without quantum resistance these days?

When Bitcoin fell to its final low of US$600 (a measure of value widely used at the time), the Bitcoin blockchain was using more electricity than China, which, at 7,000 Terawatt hours annually, consumed the most electricity of any country in the world. This had to stop and the world governments of the time, unusually, reached a consensus at the UN that the grossly inefficient Bitcoin SHA256 algorithm be banned and more efficient cryptocurrencies, depending on more economical methods and algorithms, and especially those backed by Central Banks, should take over.

This caused an outcry among organised crime syndicates and money launderers who demanded *a fair go* and the resulting *dark web* rebellions, as you will be aware, were only put down by the use of massive force in the mid-2030s. After that, the search was on to find a consensus algorithm that could stand the test of time, no matter what novel kinds of payment instruments emerged. The search itself took some considerable time.

This was the point at which Professor Sylvia Trivet made her astonishing discovery that a particular arrangement of prime numbers could be used to generate not only reliable consensus algorithms but the secure preparation of payment instructions by mental concentration alone – so called telepathic funds transfer.[5] Such instructions could not be forged and could only emanate from a single person whose identity was always traceable. Her ground-breaking paper *Prime Number Factorisation as a Substrate for Transcendental Financial Market Infrastructures*[6] was an immediate sensation, winning her the Fields Medal.

Under her leadership, the Department is continually active in research into prime number functions and the development of secure cryptographic algorithms. Her advice is widely sought after by the military industrial complex and many politicians, some shadier than others, but all shady. However, she consistently turns these offers down, committed as she is to the Institute's policy of non-violence.

Department of Creative Writing

I, Professor Somchai Rumiphilos Clarke (just call me Poong), the Chief Executive Officer of SAI, am personally responsible for the Department of Creative Writing. You may be familiar with some of my longer stories that have been made into successful films

---

5   Crude control of machines by brain computer interfaces (BCIs) was demonstrated early in the twenty-first century (see e.g., https://www.scientificamerican.com/article/new-brain-implant-turns-visualized-letters-into-text/). However, Professor Trivet was the first to apply the technique to payment systems.

6   *Acta Mathematica*, vol 73, no 14, p 320 (2047)

– not in Hollywood or Bollywood but through small studios, mainly in exotic tropical locations with a wide range of acceptable wines at reasonable prices. I am particularly happy with:

- *Plausible Deniability Never Happened*
- *Incident at the Theatre of Slime*
- *The Thermodynamics of Death*; and
- *The Actress and the Bishop are Just Good Friends*.

My major interest is in the suspension of disbelief, which emerges from an adolescent enthusiasm for science fiction (SF). How far can a creative piece go, I ask, into the realms of the extraordinary before the reader ceases to be amused and becomes unconvinced by the premise. My approach to creative writing is driven by Arthur C. Clarke's[7] Third Law: *Any sufficiently advanced technology is indistinguishable from magic.* Thus, science fiction as the most respectable branch of speculative fiction is not a matter of fantasy and especially not anything to do with the supernatural. When I see a zombie or a vampire, therefore, I reach for my gun. Not that it would do me much good in either of those cases. However, I am quite comfortable with Murakami's talking cats – you should try them.

No, SF is about the creation of experimental worlds in which speculative ideas can be explored within the bounds of what we know about human behaviour and its limitations. In teaching my students, therefore, I focus on building such worlds and making them appropriately rich and strange, as Shakespeare would say. He's still a pretty good read, as you well know.

There are times when I also indulge in a little self-reference, which is a technique in fiction that I think is under-rated. Indeed, it could be used effectively in a much wider range of situations,

---

7   No relation, as far as I am aware.

in my opinion, without giving away so much of the author's inner world that we lose that touch of mystery which adds the final chicken stock cube to the curry of life.

So, to be honest with you, I think the most creative piece of writing I have completed recently is this Prospectus.

May 2021

Kilroy Was Somewhere Else

What makes people adorn public places with some memorial of their sojourn in this tangled world? We all want to be remembered for something, but that small graffito that says, *that's me – I matter in this Universe*, is a talisman. It has the power to bestow a kind of immortality.

Maybe that's how it was for the three personalities I encountered through the single lines they left in an impetuous moment. Personalities who were determined to make their mark, not knowing whether they would be immortalised in any other way. Let's go on a journey to three widely different places and try to interpret those simple declarations of presence.

*

I was walking early one morning, which, in itself, was unusual for me. But, in the Gulf in summer, it's the only time to walk. From May onwards, midday temperatures soar to the mid-forties, so if you want to get some exercise, early is the name of the game. There are a series of attractive fountains along the Corniche in Abu Dhabi, built to honour the delegates to a Gulf Cooperation Council (GCC) conference in 1986. In a land with no water, that's pretty impressive in itself, but some of them are big things, maybe thirty feet high with refreshing liquid cascading down their sides, glinting in the sun. The Corniche bends out in an arc around each fountain, projecting just a few metres further into the sea, which moves languidly, stirring up the sand from the bottom.

I was leaning on the guard rail in front of the Volcano Fountain, the biggest of the lot, gazing out over the lagoon, benefiting from occasional droplets of cool spray. Glancing down, I saw the message, scratched in angular writing into the metal – *Fawaz the Great.*

At once striking and pathetic, the message conveyed everything in an instant. I imagined Fawaz – an Arabic name – to be a boy of about fourteen or fifteen, dressed in a brown dishdash with a bare head of dark hair. A straggly moustache is just breaking out on his upper lip. He is a boy of some intelligence. He can write perfectly good English characters, even in the tricky medium of penknife on metal railing. Maybe not a local. Perhaps the son of a settled Pakistani family with English as a first or second language, an exile from his native land, crying out for recognition. So many sub-continental people become marooned in the Gulf states, earning enough to send good money home, but not enough for the plane fare to go there too.

But not just Fawaz, the Pakistani teenager, growing up in a peaceful kind of Islam and with a passion for cricket, but Fawaz the Great. What sort of Great? Had he had a particularly good innings in a beach cricket match that day? Or did he see himself as a future conqueror of the world, like Alexander?

Maybe his family claimed descent from Alexander's forces who enjoyed their last triumphs in the Indus valley before the disastrous march to Babylon across the Gedrosian desert. Not the good or the kind, the wise, the merciful or the terrible, but the Great. Who else could he have been thinking of – an ancient or modern hero? Certainly, a hero. Only heroes are Great and only as history presents them. Those close to most Greats would perhaps prefer the epithet: *ordinary* or *late for dinner* or *never there*. But for Fawaz, heroism was the message.

And leadership. Great heroes are leaders. They march into Bactria in front of a huge army like Alexander in pursuit of Bessus. They smash a bloody path across Europe like Frederick II or Charlemagne. They save their nation from merciless invaders, like Alfred. They found huge empires, like Cyrus II. Greats are military leaders and heroes.

That was twenty years ago. But I returned a few years back and the message was still there – so a little bit of immortality achieved. But where is Fawaz now, and is he *Great*? By now, he will be in his mid-thirties perhaps. Still struggling towards respectability in the Emirates, with a wife and a few children in a small apartment. And a son who certainly regards him as *Great*. Or is he back in Pakistan with a large estate, servants, a punkah-wallah by his chair, granting audience to his many pleading relatives, to whom he is the great benefactor? Good on you, Fawaz. Be great to someone. But forget the huge army please.

*

Now we travel to the other side of the world. It is another summer day, but cooler. Much cooler. The bay stretches away to the east. The landmark bridge leaps north as the beetle-like cars cross it in droves throughout the day. The fog has cleared, and it will be a pleasant lunchtime with some colleagues, at the end of a successful week here in San Francisco.

We set out from the office towards one of the seafront restaurants where they serve lobster and the better local wines that escape export. Rabbit Run is a favourite. Looking forward to a taste of that fine liquor, we cross over the tram tracks, and I look down at the pavement, newly concreted, to be sure of my footing as the light dazzles my eyes. And there is the message: *Mr Fong goes to lunch*.

Just like us, Mr Fong, an ordinary guy going to lunch. But

an extraordinary guy. A guy who feels it necessary to mark – it looks like with his finger in wet cement – that short statement of existence for him and for the world. I am going to lunch. So, damn you all. I will not be dictated to by some boss – I don't care if I get fired. I am going to lunch! Was it like that – the emotions anger and pride? I will decide what I do! He throws down his chef's hat and walks out of the sweaty kitchen.

Or maybe an assertion by a successful man? I have finished my task. I have completed what I aimed to do today. I have been patted on the back by my client. I am a respected man – MISTER Fong to you. And with that, the luggage of the past is dispensed with. No longer a despised immigrant, here to serve the gold rush, build the railways, to suffer and die in the pitiless work gangs driving the tracks through the Rockies. No. I have made it. I am Mr Fong, and I am going to lunch. I will relax, smoke a small cigar, drink a glass of good wine and have some fish head soup – my favourite. He is in his early forties, smart, wearing a tie and a grey suit. The lunch is good.

There is another scenario though, isn't there? Mr Fong is a capricious and unpredictable boss, feared by his staff, hated by his competitors. Only this morning, Fong, smoking a huge cigar and sitting with his feet up on the desk, calls in the chief accountant, roars at her and demands nationwide sales figures to be on his desk by noon.

"We will go through them," he barks as only American managers can. "And they better be good. I got stock options riding on 'em!"

The team works all morning, calling 171 branches for a flash report. Alice, the accountant, shaking with fear and expecting a bad case of shooting the messenger, brings the figures to his office at 11.55. He is not there.

"Oh, he's gone to lunch," states his PA with certainty. "Back at three o'clock."

Alice storms back to her office, at least as stormily as a meek accountant can, shuts her door and bursts into tears. After a couple of minutes, Mr Lim, the old bookkeeper, knocks gingerly on the door and steps into the room.

"Fong is not worth upsetting yourself for, Alice. Besides, in our community, we can fix him. I have one of the boys out there now leaving a message for him. He will be no problem this afternoon."

At 2.30, Fong steps out of the restaurant in a self-satisfied mood. As he crosses the small service road outside, he spots it. Clear and unmistakable, chiselled into the paving. A coded curse: *Mr Fong goes to lunch.* He is horrified – who could have done this? He is distracted and walks on, staring back over his shoulder just to be sure. He hears a bell, turns too fast and stumbles into the main street – into the path of an oncoming tram.

It was undeniable. Mr Fong would not be a problem that afternoon.

*

Another hot country, but not a hot time of year. It is December in Greece. Attica. I am about forty kilometres outside Athens on a windy headland overlooking the blue Aegean. Ferries plough a path through the sea heading for Piraeus, or down to Naxos, Mykonos or Crete. From this hilltop, King Aegeus cast himself down into the crashing waves, believing the worst, as he saw the ship of his son Theseus returning from Crete but still carrying a black sail. Theseus, being somewhat preoccupied with a couple of complicated ladies, had forgotten to change the sail to a white one, signalling that he had won his duel with the Minotaur.

So, the sea was named after Aegeus and the hilltop dedicated to Poseidon, bad-tempered God of the sea and storms. One of the most evocative temples in all of Greece – the Temple of Poseidon – is here at Cape Sounion. It's one of the most romantic places on earth, even as a ruin. And one of the most scrawled over. There are thousands of etched graffiti on the temple. They go back mainly to the nineteenth century when the rest of Europe was starting to rediscover Greece. The traditional sites in Italy had become less accessible because of the Napoleonic Wars and the Grand Tourists found their way to the ancient Greek sites instead.

But there is one graffito in particular that I am looking for. And there it is, low down on a square pillar at the back of the structure. A single word, slightly emphasised by the stone being a little cleaner than those around it: *Byron*.

In contrast to Fawaz and Mr Fong, we know a lot about George Gordon, Lord Byron and his love affair with Greece. Most only know about his tragi-comic excursion into the Greek War of Independence, where he died of fever at Messolonghi on the north west corner of the Gulf of Corinth before he could get anywhere near the fighting, but not before he had spent a small fortune training worthless troops, who he finally sent home on the very day he became seriously ill in February 1824. Some say he suffered the evil eye, not because of ill-will, but because of the desire of a young woman who caught his gaze as he walked from his ship, already dogged by failing health.

However, there is a lesser-known tale to tell. Some years before the revolution broke out, he had travelled extensively in Greece, ostensibly gathering ancient manuscripts from Byzantine monasteries. It was probably at this time that he carved his memorial into the stone at Sounion.

The story of his visit to Greece is intriguing. He had become interested by the myths, if they are myths, of the Dionysian festivals of the Maenads – legendary women who lured men to their rites, had their wicked way with them and then tore them to pieces as offerings to the God of chaos, and the great Goddess. In the early nineteenth century, perhaps as an echo of the earlier hermetic revivals, eccentric English aristocrats were not averse to a little Bacchic frenzy with whatever wild women were available... as long as there was a reasonable chance of escape.

Byron and his entourage had gone up into the mountains to explore whatever rituals could be located at the right time of year. Maybe it was returning from a wild night in the mountains that Byron decided he must make his mark in stone? Or maybe on his way there and wondering whether he would return in one piece...or more?

For a romantic poet, being torn apart by beautiful women would have been an acceptable death. Certainly, better than being carted off by a bacterium and losing your glimpse of glory.

*

But where would I leave my mark? I think not on stone, concrete, or steel. I think I would prefer to be engraved on a heart or two. And so, I have taken many beautiful women to Sounion, but only one ever kissed me there.

Fortunately, it was the right one.

October 2007

An Evening at Table 10

Bucharest, March 2003

Iancu gazed out of the first-floor window of The Harp, watching the snow fall in the gentle orange glow of the sodium lights. It was good that he had managed to grab Table 10, the only one with a view. Battered Dacia's lurched by like dull-coated rabbits scurrying for their burrows. The huge square of Piazza Unirii was pretty at night, especially after a winter snowfall. Crumbling concrete buildings adorned with fresh-lit signage; the hedges and worn grass fresh-painted in white.

A wise-eyed waitress had arrived with the first round and talk had begun. After such a hard week, Iancu merely wanted to sit back, listen and drink. He had no energy even to inspect the clientele or imagine who might have the sweetest kiss or the warmest embrace. It was Friday night, thank God. His strenuous act of command as Team Leader could rest for a short while.

His companions were a strange crew, brought together for the purpose of introducing modern ways in this emerging land and providing the tools for change and growth. Romania had a lot to do before it could join in the affluence and comfort of its European cousins in the West. Meanwhile, beer was a dollar a pint. Here was Lloyd Denton, the American, full of enthusiasm and confidence and political correctness; Maria Kalamatianou, the Greek economist, cool, red-lipped and distracted; Mike Mallet the Brit, ex-para, practical, tough and inscrutable, with the same intelligent wariness you see in the eyes of a gorilla.

Before coming down to the Irish bar, Kalamatianou had

listened to the latest on Showdown Iraq on CNN. Bush was posturing like the hero of a bad B-movie, she declared. Blair had led a group of EU premiers to sign a letter urging support for the sabre-rattling coalition. Papandreou, the Greek foreign minister – in the EU Chair for these crucial months – was being critical, urging restraint and a peaceful solution. Kalamatianou was dismissive.

"*Malakas*!" Wankers! "I despair of good sense among men. If only women ruled, peace would be the natural order of things. Why don't you men grow out of playing at Stone Age warriors? You are incapable of making decisions that can bring about the peaceful aims of the Union. Don't you find it funny that the French and Germans together are urging peace?" She drew harshly on a cigarette and blew smoke at Mallet who waved it away with a chuckle.

"How come so many beautiful women smoke?" he asked in a smooth tone. Kalamatianou leaned forward to deliver the full force of her eyes.

"Because it's sexy."

Denton heard it and laughed guardedly, as the music was turned up a notch.

Although he found the confidence of his female colleague's reply strikingly attractive, Iancu pointedly changed the subject.

"What do you think makes Irish bars such a success?" he asked. "Did you know there's one in Moscow airport? It's been there since the changes in '91. Just like the real thing except you can pay in dollars. Hey, let's order some food, I'm starving. I will pick some of the best Romanian dishes for you – *ciorba de vacutsa, sarmale* and *mamaliga*, some lamb." There were murmurs of assent.

Iancu shifted his gaze back to the window, hoping that the party could get through the evening without a major flare up between Denton and Mallet over the Iraqi situation. Romanians were sick of politics. It was getting them nowhere, other than that the shops were less empty, there was enough to eat and the city was full of foreign advisers spending money, and, of course, you could say what you wanted without fear of the secret police. So maybe they were getting somewhere? He smiled wryly to himself.

Iancu would go home to his cosy two-room apartment on Unirii Boulevard, while the three foreigners shared a place nearer the centre of town around Piazza Victoria. Iancu liked going there as it was spacious and modern, but he was always intrigued by the sight of the three of them sitting together in the living room, all with laptop computers open on their knees and BBC World, Euronews or CNN going full blast on the TV. It was a companionable state, and he sometimes brought his own work just to join in. He couldn't afford the laptop, but would be able to soon if he got another contract like this. Iancu knew he had to keep in with this crowd. Tonight, though, he had to keep the conversation light and the Iraqi topic was not going to help.

Intellectually, Mallet was easily underestimated. He was a joker, a card, a ladies' man. On the topic of conflict though, Iancu could almost see him changing into a higher gear. He switched off his normal cruise control and began to slice elegantly through the logic of the situation. Iancu suddenly realised why Mallet got these jobs – he was clear, incisive, reliable. Or was there more to it than that? Did his strength of mind disguise his real role in this situation? If he was risking blowing a cover, though, there must be a good reason.

Mallet began.

"Look, Lloyd, me ol' mate. Let me give you an example. It's like me saying to you there's a pink rabbit behind you but you're not allowed to look. What counts as evidence that there's a pink rabbit, eh? None of these American officials can tell us who these pink rabbits are, what they are planning to do, whether they are capable of doing it. *Hidden network of cold-blooded killers*, says Bush-baby. They've been on orange alert for months and nothing has happened. Crying wolf, maybe? Maybe the rabbits aren't pink after all. Maybe someone, matey, is trying to wind someone up. Don't you think?"

Iancu's first thought was, how does Saddam's Iraq compare with what Ceausescu did here? The half-truths, the insinuations, the climate of fear. He had been an admirable leader for a few years – no foreign debt, an active economy, everyone had jobs and there was enough food in the shops. But after a while he became capricious. He violently put down any opposition and turned into a narcissistic showman, brokering dodgy deals with Gadhafi in Libya just to spite both the West and the Soviets. What had been true in the national statistics turned to wishful thinking and the downward spiral began. In the end it was really his henchmen who ousted him and who were now still in power under a nominal democracy. There are always conspiracies – dark bargains made in smoky hotel rooms by powerful men.

Kalamatianou rocked back on her chair, flicked her hair and laughed.

"*Apolytos*! Absolutely! No sign of any violent incident, but a few centimetres of snow in Washington last week caused more disruption than any terrorists have managed for years." Her red-glossed lips passed a smile to Mallet, which struck Iancu as conspiratorial. "In any case, the inspectors have found nothing substantial. It's just rumours."

Denton was floored for an instant but came up punching.

"Inspectors are auditors, not detectives. They're just checking what the Iraqis actually have in the stockpiles, like they did in

South Africa. The Iraqis say they've come clean, but what's the truth? To be sure, we've got to get rid of the guy."

Before Mallet could open up, Kalamatianou snapped back, still blowing smoke.

"Why not just containment? It's a better solution than a war, which would cause devastation and destabilise the region. The West would just end up with a much bigger terrorist threat. Why make things even more unpredictable by changing the devil you know for devils you don't? Seems like opening Pandora's box to me."

Mallet chimed in.

"Inspections are an impossible way to get at truth. They're just like asking the Iraqis 'Where haven't you got Weapons of Mass Destruction, so we can go there and not see them?'"

Denton saw a chance. "Then you're agreeing with me. We've got to get rid of the guy. Then we can go in and find out the truth."

Mallet shook his head as if contradicting a child.

"So, we spend ten years combing thirty million square miles of Iraqi desert and we find bugger all. What then? We say sorry and move out? Having wasted trillions, killed hundreds of thousands and stitched up their economy for decades? You're bloody joking, mate – the scandal would undermine all the values we're trying to promote. Ninety per cent, Saddam is bluffing and the information we're being fed is just so you Yanks can punish the bloke for selling his oil in euros instead of dollars."

Denton wasn't giving in.

"What about democracy? We'll bring democracy. Can't you see that's what they need?" he insisted, abandoning his previous line of argument.

Mallet almost snarled.

"I can think of a few places, ol' son, that could clean up their own act before trying to export their form of government." He caught the waitress's eye as she delivered the hot dishes and changed the subject to the next round of drinks.

Denton turned to Iancu.

"The trouble with Brits is they don't understand the past and how it hits you when you least expect it."

Iancu remembered with a jolt the private conversation they had shared earlier in the project, and he knew Denton recalled it too. For Denton, the past was Vietnam. His brother had died there, cut down by a VC sniper at the edge of a swamp. He had explained to Iancu that every time he thought of it, the back of his throat swelled as he held back the sea of emotion the memory evoked. His brother, twelve years older, had taught him everything about being a young man in the sixties. Stuff his dad didn't understand – rock music, tuning up old cars, impressing girls. His brother had taken him to a beach to see girls in skimpy bikinis. He couldn't believe what he was seeing and had to limp back to the car doubled over. Now, after all those deaths, the waters had closed over that piece of history and there was a McDonald's in Saigon. He refused to think of it as Ho Chi Minh City. And the Brits were not there.

America's shame began in Vietnam, Denton had explained. Then the fearsome mess of Somalia, the ongoing struggle in Afghanistan diluting what had seemed like a victory. Only Desert Storm was a bright spot – throwing the damned Iraqis out of Kuwait, seeing that vast convoy of Iraqi armour strafed to a bloody standstill on the desert highway. Denton was no redneck, he insisted to Iancu, but it was time for America to show it was not a nation of pansies, that it could police the world, send in the cavalry and smash the bad guy. Iancu was not convinced, but he had let the remarks go and nodded sagely.

As Denton waved away the option of another beer, Iancu was concerned that this conversation was becoming destructive. Mallet was risking Denton's terrors coming to the surface, by being unknowingly insensitive.

Denton was clearly irritated with Mallet's sniping and seemed to be keeping his cool only for the sake of their team objectives. A broken team at this point in the project would be bad news. Iancu was constantly on edge about delivering a consensus report in the next fortnight. He recalled the Vietnam conversation again. Denton was at breaking point. Why couldn't Mallet see it – but then Mallet didn't know about the past. Or was there something more?

"Hey, you're quiet, Yank." Mallet pushed the emotional buttons again. The conversation had been flowing around Denton as he gazed out of the window at the snow, appearing haunted by his own thoughts. "Don't tell me you really believe this stuff about Weapons of Mass Destruction?"

"If Colin Powell believes it, why not?" Denton slashed back. "Your baby, Blair, is in, isn't he?"

"He's just a politician, mate. What does he know about war? He's just brown-nosing the US establishment expecting favours later!"

"The US doesn't trade favours in wars," snapped Denton, unconvincingly.

"Look, mate, don't talk to me about what happens in wars. I don't talk about it much, but remember that I was in the Falklands and in Belfast. Situations get out of control; bullets are fired more in terror than cool calculation. Then the trading starts, I assure you – bureaucrats rather than soldiers decide the rights and wrongs. And the press has more influence on people's understanding than the truth that can never be told. Don't be naïve, matey. Your lot do the same backroom deals with armed groups to keep some sort of hope going."

Iancu knew that Mallet was a realist and could foresee plenty of risk in a jingoistic, glory-seeking mother of all battles provoked by an angry, idealistic superpower searching for validation on the thinnest of excuses. That was the antithesis of Denton's view of things.

*

As Iancu silently demolished a plate of *sarmale* and *mamaliga*, he tried to work out how to defuse the conversation. He was still worrying about the report they had to deliver. It had to be clear, decisive, unambiguous, so that the powers that be could not back away from the conclusion that Romania needed to spend plenty on infrastructure if it were to get near to EU membership any time soon. And the controls to avoid and punish corruption had to be firmly in place to make it work.

Was Mallet trying to undermine the chance to get a clean report delivered? It was Denton and Kalamatianou who were the real subject matter experts. Mallet was their security and logistics manager, but what was he really here for? Denton was looking for conspiracies in far off governments, but Iancu wondered about something closer to home. On the other hand, he admired the Greek lady, who seemed to think that Denton and Mallet were just silly little boys. Maybe she was right.

As Iancu finished his meal, he tuned in to the conversation again. Denton was saying something pompous about the UN enforcing its own resolutions, and that bullies like Saddam only understood force. Mallet regarded this argument as too simplistic, especially since most European governments could see through the weakness of Powell's evidence.

Denton shifted ground again. "But the Iraqi regime is in bed with Al Qaeda and other extremist terrorist groups. After 9/11, Americans are right to be on the attack, break down the restrictions that weak countries at the UN try to impose – neighbours are scared that the Islamic terrorist might be next door."

Kalamatianou broke in.

"What evidence does anyone have that the regime in Iraq or North Korea or anywhere has links with those who pervert Islam. Do you have it? They haven't produced anything credible. What did the inspectors find? Nothing material. A few missiles that go 160 kilometres instead of 150 kilometres. A few empty shells. What does it mean? How can you justify invading a sovereign country because you don't much like its leader or how it treats its people? It's the thin end of a dangerous wedge."

"Yeah," Mallet cut in, uncurling from fiddling with his wallet. "William Roper...mate, 'I'd cut down every law in England to get after the devil!' Remember Thomas More's response? Of course you don't, you're a bloody Yank. He said, 'And when the last law was down, and the devil turned round on you, where would you hide?'"

Like William Roper, Denton had no answer to this.

"Ah, you don't understand. You don't see how we feel in the States after 9/11."

Mallet's cool exterior bubbled a bit, like paint in the sun.

"And you don't understand how we feel in London after thirty years of bombs and hoaxes, largely financed by people in New York. Standing night after night in the rain outside Victoria Station. So, we should nuke New York, should we?"

Kalamatianou flicked her cigarette into the ashtray. Iancu saw her glance at the two combatants. "Silly little boys," she muttered. He was glad to be excluded from that remark. She looked at him intensely for a couple of seconds, then closed her eyes momentarily.

"You men are always the ones with the conflicts. What gives any of you the right to settle someone else's battle by force. What happens? What happens! Every violent action begets another violent action. Wars can never be justified. And wars with no UN backing? They are just a question of invading another country because maybe you have some commercial aims – oil maybe? Mallet's right, you know. Not often, but this time." She smiled openly at him, as she lit another cigarette.

"Mind you." Mallet grinned, knowing how this would raise the temperature even more. "If there's one regime that needs changing it's the one in Israel."

Denton swore under his breath, as the waitress bent down to sweep up some empty glasses.

Iancu turned from the window, deciding it was time to break up the party. "Well," he said, "day off tomorrow, my good friends. But we all need to relax. Maybe it's time to call it a night." Mallet followed his lead and stood up.

"Yeah, let's get to bed…maybe even get to sleep."

Iancu noticed a look between Mallet and Kalamatianou and felt a rush of jealousy. He decided to drive the three of them back to the apartment and remind Mallet that there were rules – no relationships within the team. He managed it discreetly enough by referring to an incident from a couple of years ago as they walked cautiously across the icy pavement to the car. Mallet was the soul of prudence.

"Don't worry, mate, we were all a bit airy tonight. I've already apologised to Lloyd for implying that the US is sinking in debt and about to crash. But you know me, ol' mate – I'm a Brit, I can be subtle when I need to be."

It took quite a while to get to the apartment through the snowy night, crammed into Iancu's basic Aro 4-wheel drive. The American went to his room as soon as they got in, professing tiredness. The others said they'd watch the news before they turned in. Iancu declared he would sleep on the sofa as it had begun to snow again.

*

Denton slept fitfully, thinking about the deaths in Vietnam. At one point, he thought he heard a noise, almost a moan, from somewhere and five minutes later a click like a door closing. He turned over and began to cry.

March 2003

The Detonations in Freud's Bookcase

In those moments lying in the dark, perhaps with a hand to hold, or perhaps without, I find myself exploring the mental sleight of hand that allows me to maintain some semblance of conscious control over my existence, even though I am aware that most of my actions are determined unconsciously. A game of cards played by the soul, if there is one. I muse on who is at the table.

I recall the story of a discussion between the psychoanalysts Sigmund Freud and Carl Jung that took place in Freud's home, in Vienna, I believe. The discussion concerned, on the one hand, the curious set of phenomena collectively termed Extra Sensory Perception (ESP) and, on the other hand, and at another level of discourse, the relationship between the two men. Freud, it seems, being the older of the two, was a father-figure to Jung who nonetheless wished to convince his senior of the veracity of ESP phenomena. Freud was sceptical.

Deep in conversation, Jung declares that he believes a loud sound will emanate from a cupboard in the room. The cupboard contains books. Within seconds, an explosive report issues from the bookcase, amenable to no obvious or subtle explanation. The bookcase is examined for damage, but none is found. The discussion continues.

Freud remains cynical, unprepared to admit signs and wonders in evidence of physical processes, but Jung declares the likelihood of a recurrence of the disturbing auditory event. Again, a detonation occurs, apparently without cause, or indeed effect, on the bookcase. The effect on the two men, however, is different. A wedge is, as it were, driven between them for, while Jung is further convinced of the processes of ESP, Freud is thrown back on coincidence and begins to mistrust his colleague. "He who has ears to hear, let him hear."

But that is not all.

What of another experience of Jung's, where, while interviewing a patient with regard to her dream, a surprising event occurs? The lady's dream, it appears, concerns a scarab design, which is also to be found on the back of certain African beetles. There is a tapping at the window and perched on the sill, attempting to enter the room, is an example of the nearest European equivalent to the African scarab beetle.

So, what are we to conclude? Do we suppose, like Freud, that all such events are statistical variations? The extreme variance from the mean. The unlikely occurrence, which is so unlikely that it becomes appropriate. We ask: *How often do scarabs appear at Jung's window?* and *Do the detonations in Freud's bookcase also occur under other circumstances?* This is the analysis of causal relationships between events, explicable in terms of physical science.

Or do we suppose, with Jung, that these are examples of ESP? The scarab is caused to fly at the window by the thoughts of dreamer and analyst, which somehow attract it. Either the detonations occur as a direct result of Jung wishing them to occur to illustrate his point, or both events – the wish and the report – occur as a result of some larger cause that we might term a *great process in the sky.*

But on the third hand, supposing we had one, in this card game of coincidence, we may admit a further explanation and, as is the case in other dichotomies of scientific thought, the third way combines the first and the second in such a manner that it is different in kind from either of them.

Let us take another example, one in which the illusion of cause and effect is not so apparent. A couple have occasion to attend a large function at a well-known hotel in London. They enjoy the meal, which for a gathering of a hundred people or more is pretty good. In the latter part of the evening, they get up to dance. In the course of this terpsichorean interlude the wife loses a contact lens from her right eye. It is never found.

The next year, at the same function, at the same time in the evening, the event is repeated exactly.

The *great process in the sky* might be invoked to *cause* both events, but one could not be said to cause the other, although one might suggest that the memory of the first event predisposed the conditions for the second. Is there a framework of ideas that enables us to comprehend events of this type, we may enquire? Let us, then, invoke a philosopher to hold the third hand and suppose Arthur Koestler is seated at our card table of coincidence.

The third hand is played. Koestler proposes an acausal process in the universe, a unifying principle, the principle of confluent events. Here is a description of coincidence that is perhaps also an elegant solution. But what is the nature of such a process? Does it have an origin or a purpose, either created or evolutionary?

And now, as you read these lines, a further thought may occur to you. How appropriate it is, you may remark to yourself, to be reading this tale at this instant. For was it not only yesterday or the day before that so-and-so happened to mention such-and-such an event of this very nature? And you may think of me as you do of the newspaper astrologer whose mystic pronouncements have an inordinate ring of credibility about them, despite their very high chance of being nothing more than guesses.

How did he know? What explanation can there be?

Oh, I forgot – for it all to feel plausible, to engage your emotions, dear reader, in a way that a conjurer only a metre away can instantiate something as material as a rabbit before your very eyes, a trump must have been played. And who could be playing the fourth hand but someone who can dissolve the barriers between reality and fantasy without disrupting your suspension of disbelief.

Jorge Luis Borges perhaps? I recall Borges' story *The Zahir* – concerning a coin about which the hero becomes fixated. Whatever he does, he cannot forget the Zahir. It dominates his thoughts, his actions, his intentions. It is an allegory both of romantic and clinical obsession. Borges plays with the themes of metaphysics, the structure of reality and, in 'The Garden of Forking Paths', with labyrinths embodying an infinite series of times, diverging and parallel.

Suddenly, we can see the questions that have to be faced. What led the two psychologists to be together at that moment in a universe in which the coincidence of the detonation – if it was one – were to occur? Where was the scarab beetle on its way to when it encountered Jung's window? What is the question whose answer is 'you cannot know'?

And so, as I lie here in the dark, in deep satisfaction and yet overwhelming anxiety, perhaps existing in an infinite number of universes where all possible outcomes of all possible actions exist, I meditate on whether there can be a winner or loser in this endless video game we call life. In reality, it is only how we feel that exists. We are actors and observers of events in each other's lives, the quintessence of which we can never experience.

January 1977

Acknowledgements

First of all, I have to thank my long-term friend and colleague Dr Richard Skinner for his encouragement to get these stories published, and for the great fun we have had over the years writing and performing cabaret and working on philosophical issues around science and religion. Richard has provided invaluable editorial input into the stories, and it was he who made the connection for me with SilverWood Books for which I am most grateful.

I would also like to give a mention to Gary Rutland, former scion of the independent record industry in Canada, music critic and my cycling buddy in Thailand. Gary gave me some helpful editorial suggestions as well as being instrumental in getting me to focus more on writing and finding a way to get my stories read by a wider public. Gary is an able writer himself who runs two Facebook groups, the exciting music site *Radio Rutland* and *Now Read This!* in which I hope *Someone Else's Gods* will feature in due course.

My editor, Lesley Hart, has provided highly valuable assistance in helping me to polish the stories from a professional point of view, ensuring I manage sensitivities that might otherwise get me into trouble, and teaching me how to avoid the literary crime of 'head-hopping'.

Helen Hart and her team at SilverWood Books have been professional, supportive and helpful. I feel I have learned an enormous amount through the publishing journey and that the next time will be even more enriching. I'm reminded of the fact that all parents are amateurs when they have their first child. I remember that experience well and there are striking parallels in nurturing a first book into print.

To my Thai wife, Tue, who has looked after me throughout the strange times in which we live, delivering, unbidden, innumerable quantities of coffee, tea and support. I offer my grateful thanks.

And thanks also to those unsung heroes who have inspired many of the characters and events in the stories. Although all are fictional, it is often those little human incidents and chance meetings that set off a train of thought that leads to the creation of a narrative and breathes life into a personality. Maybe some of them will strike a chord with you.

Forthcoming Publications by Gordon R Clarke

Creative Tales

Gordon R Clarke's second collection of short stories takes the themes of *Someone Else's Gods* further into the realm of speculative fiction, while remaining firmly grounded in the psychology of humanity. We meet again some familiar characters: the lovely Samantha with her blistering Christmas letters, Simon, the most pan-dimensional salesman in Singapore, and his resistant victim, Mike. We meet Miles, the writer of raunchy novels, and Milos, the proprietor of the 'Theatre of Slime'. We look again into the future with a letter to a grandchild, and into the past with another archaeological discovery, a long letter concerning the ill-fated Symposium of Grecas, from which the following extract is taken.

Symposium

Minutes of the Cambridge Hellenic History Society 2 July 2012.
Business of the meeting: Presentation of the translation of a recently recovered manuscript from the Ptolemaic Era.
Presenter: Dr Tina Rawlinson, recently appointed Director of the Institute for Graeco-Roman Studies.

*

It is not well known that ancient urban society was by no means concerned with the same cultural norms and conventions as we experience in the modern West. In particular, the tradition of monogamy and the, relatively modern, idea of the nuclear family were not the norm in, for example, the post-Alexandrine societies of Greece, the Levant and Ptolemaic Egypt. These were patriarchal societies in which the expectations and responsibilities placed on senior men in society were substantial, and failing to meet those expectations could result in severe punishment. The fate of Socrates is a case in point. The worst fear perhaps was banishment from the city and its institutions – to be 'ostracised'. Such sanctions could be very sudden, as a result of a misplaced choice of friends or opinions, or any suspicion of connivance with the enemy powers that were always out there, on the edge, in the dark.

In the late 1990s, a letter was discovered in almost perfect condition, with the exception of, tantalisingly, the opening section. This part was damaged, thus preventing the intention of the letter from being entirely clear. The letter was written in the Greek of Ptolemaic Egypt. The manuscript was encoded, in the form of a papyrus ribbon which must be wrapped around a cylinder in order to be read. The material can be dated to 200–190 BCE, although this does not confirm that the letter was actually composed at that time. It was found in a ceramic jar buried in fifteen feet of sand in the Negev desert not far from modern Aqaba. How it came to be there remains unclear, but it may be that the writer was in exile there, or that his correspondent lived there.

The writer was a Hellenistic nobleman named Grecas, about whom there appears to be no other historical reference. The letter appears to be written to an acquaintance unfamiliar with the cultural activities of classical Greek society. References to Greek activity in Egypt date the letter to after the time of Alexander the Great, and a lack of references to the Roman occupation of Egypt and the demise of the Ptolemies with Cleopatra VII, imply that it was before the incursions of the first century BCE. Mention of Philip V of Macedon can be taken to confirm a more precise timeframe of around the end of the second century BCE.

I have reproduced the translation here as a complete document and will walk through it on the screen. I am happy to provide the material, in confidence, to members after this meeting, as I would be keen to hear your interpretations. As you will see, there are a number of references and events that will require considerable scholarship to unravel.

*

...wish for your...as I have no longer the...sudden change in circumstances...safety of my...in this place although comfortable at present...unknown risks. My few companions provide me with all the necessary support but...astonishing events which I will attempt to relate.

In our society, men have always considered themselves the focal point of intellectual endeavour, and the seat of power. Ever since, that is, the defeat of the Amazons and the Maenads, who may still lurk somewhere in the woods, not far from Delphi. For woman is comely in form and gentle in spirit, while man is rough and strong and full of passion. Man leads in war and politics, woman in the home, ordering the servants and the children, warming the heart of man when he returns from the stresses of the hunt, the agora and the battle. Is that not how things have always been? Since the defeat of the Amazons and the Maenads.

About a month ago at my home in Elath, not far from the ancient port of King Solomon at Ezion Geber, I held a Symposium, which I had been planning for some months. You may not be aware that a Symposium involves not only discussion of philosophical matters, but also entertainment both musical and dramatic and, of course, much eating and drinking. The entertainment is designed for the pleasure of men and it is normal that no ladies take part in the proceedings directly other than the flute girls and the ladies of the household.

I have three wives and they organised the proceedings together, as they always do for me. Martia cooks, for she is a genius at the hearth. Prescani organises the entertainment, for she is a former flute girl herself and knows how to negotiate with strong women. Ancilla ensures all goes smoothly with the household and engaged servants, that all food and drink will be served on time, that vomit will be quickly cleaned away and any other bodily fluids dealt with expeditiously. They are all a man could desire. When the home is secure, the formidable forces of the city can be kept at bay at least for a night. Or so I believed.

Before the proceedings began, the children were brought before me. There are eight at present and Prescani is again pregnant with her fourth. They are my pride and I love them all so much. Grecas Marcus and Grecas Cretus who will carry my name and those of their godfathers, the beautiful Marcelli and Vrelli, now fourteen and fifteen, respectively, and already the target of many suitors, all of whom I have seen off unceremoniously. The twins, little Semis and Telis, so happily playing together on a bearskin rug before the hearth. The rug was a present from my cousin Melos, from the mountains, where the bears are plentiful and dangerous. Simona and Dimitris are away. They are grown now and making their own way. Thracis, Simona's husband, knows the subtle arts of reading the poetry of the signs. Dimitris is at the frontier, with our Syrian cousins, guarding against Scythian raiders. We only hear from him every month or so and the silence is distressing as it wears on. But we received a package from him yesterday, so both I and Martia, his mother, were feeling relieved.

To Prescani and Ancilla, he is like a brother and they also love him and fear for his safety. Ancilla received the package and brought it to my study with joy. She sat on my lap and kissed my head as we opened the packages, which contained a letter and a jewelled box for Vrelli, for the day of her god. Ancilla is very loving. Some of my friends ask me how I manage to keep three women satisfied. It is not so difficult when they are so determined to please. Am I a lucky man or has my choice been wise and my care equitable as the gods demand? For if a man is true to his values and kind but firm to his family all blessings will be given by nature and men.

And so, on the propitious date set by the reading of the poetry of the signs and other oracles, the formalities of the Symposium commenced – the food laid out, the wine prepared, the flute girls and other entertainers ready to begin their performances. As the sword of Orion emerged above the sparkling sea-horizon, the guests began to arrive.

How tragic that such a joyous and propitious occasion should end in such unforeseen events. For reasons that will become obvious, my dear friend, I will not vouchsafe to you the list of guests, for it could endanger their lives.

*

The Long-Distance Executioner

Gordon R Clarke's novella *The Long-Distance Executioner* echoes the alienation of Sillitoe's long-distance runner. However, in this story, the anti-hero is not a downtrodden class victim, but an educated middle-class man who has succeeded in carrying out an insanely dangerous plot – a plot that could change the destiny of nations. And yet he is far from insane and knows that every event has determined consequences. He will always be a marked man, an outlaw destined for punishment, if only those seeking to bring him to their own kind of justice can identify him and locate his remote hiding place. Meanwhile a professional assassin is also stalking him, not to destroy him but to recruit him into a deadly game as old as civilisation.

*

"Assassination is the extreme form of censorship" – George Bernard Shaw (*The Shewing-Up of Blanco Posnet* (1911) 'Limits to Toleration')

(1)

John Selby. It was not the name of an assassin. Not a Fawkes or a Booth, a Ruby or a Sirhan. Just a plain English name, signifying nothing. He looked at his hands. They were not a murderer's hands. Long-fingered, clean, neatly manicured. He was not wearing the clothes of a killer. No blood or torn cloth, no smell of cordite, no stain of DNA.

But he had done it. After months of meticulous planning,

painstaking research, watching his quarry's habits, favourite haunts and routes, watching his bodyguards and recording their weaknesses, studying social and political calendars for the best opportunity, he had done it. And as far as he could tell, he had got away with it. The police appeared baffled, as one by one the usual suspects had been interrogated and then released. That could be a cover, of course, as political executions would not go unpunished, any more than murders of police officers. Eventually, someone would have to be charged – and convicted. But he had left the country apparently unobserved and the tropical beach he was now walking on, as the sun descended towards the sea after a pleasantly warm afternoon, was deserted, apart from two fat ladies walking coiffured little dogs. No sirens, no rapidly approaching footsteps, no threatening cries.

He sat down on a half-buried packing case washed up on the shore and gazed at the horizon. The beach was long and flat, backed by grassland, with a few ramshackle beach bars. The odd fishing boat had been hauled out for repairs and a lone carpenter scraped away at a replaced wooden beam. Gulls screeched overhead as the sun dived towards the horizon throwing up a blaze of colour.

Selby was coming to terms with events but knew his life would never be the same. He felt numb rather than worried and knew it would take a while before he was emotionally composed again. When he separated from his wife two years earlier, he had received half the proceeds of the house sale and had some minor investments that generated a small income – nothing like enough to live in England, but manageable here on an ex-colonial coast where language was not an issue. He had rented a flat on a two-year lease, but once the hubbub had tailed off, he would spend a few weeks back in the UK, would unexpectedly leave his job in the record industry and then, only then, disappear. No one knew where he was and, perhaps after a few years, if things had calmed down, he could get back in touch with friends and cousins and invite them to visit him in paradise. This place would remove any questions as to his sudden departure. It was hugely more attractive than rain-sodden Hertfordshire.

It was not easy to smile though, and hard to keep his distance from enquiring voices in the bars of an evening. He had never been a big drinker, but now had to maintain the persona of a holidaying Brit without, even once, letting his guard down. Fortunately, his bar companions were mainly Russians, preoccupied with their own affairs and unaware of the furore he had brought about in his native land. Selby could drink and read alone with few questions asked.

*

In Westminster, however, such peace was far from the Prime Minister's state of mind. He had taken the news of the assassination – or murder as the press labelled it – with curiously mixed feelings. The victim was Sir Maurice Ambrose. He had been knighted on the PM's recommendation for services to something or other, on the understanding that he would shut up and go away. He hadn't. Instead, he had become a dangerous political rival with an extreme and violent viewpoint, often leaving the PM red-faced and spluttering on talk shows. He appealed massively to an underclass left for dead by the break-up of the Union. He was the populists' populist with a party now becoming coherent, disciplined, and unpleasantly aggressive. To anyone but those desperate for a leader in devastating times, he was a ranting, ignorant demagogue, the kind that is easy to follow down the primrose path to hell. Transparently corrupt, transparently hot-headed, but wretchedly inspiring.

In the PM's view, there was more than a fleeting consideration of *He had it coming.* On the other hand, the PM's political credibility was wearing thin after seven lacklustre years on the job, in the wake of the Union partition. It had crossed his mind more than once that keeping on the right side of Ambrose could do him some good in terms of sustaining his grip on power and, of course, the personal benefits, shall we say, that go along with it in the shambling wreck of a once great nation.

Nevertheless, rabble rousers are seldom welcome on anyone's political playing field, and especially not at this time when a period of upheaval seemed to be calming down. But three weeks on, with no credible group claiming responsibility for the gruesome death and no suspects, other politicos were getting jumpy. Who would be next? The PM was thinking of terror groups such as the Greek Revolutionary Organization 17 November (17N) who had declared themselves to be white knights purging the world of corruption, with more than a score of murders. But when they were eventually unmasked after a bungled plot, they proved to be just a small gang of dissolute armed robbers that had long ago lost what principles they might once have had. Nevertheless, they had Athens running scared for nearly thirty years. It was never proven whether their rumoured high political links were real or not.

A group like that operating in England would be bad news – really bad – for the administration. And what if it was a foreign plot, handing the nationalist ranters a cause célèbre? On the other hand, it could give just the excuse needed for more surveillance, more money to be spent on police and army, and a potential vote-winner if people could be kept scared. But every silver-lining has its cloud, and the PM was due for some tough questioning in Parliament today about the lack of progress on the case.

(2)

Sir Maurice Ambrose had not expected to die that day when he got out of bed. He had dressed and breakfasted as usual, barked some instructions to his wife, Doris, about an event in the evening and set off for the forty-minute trip to his office in his chauffeured Mercedes. On the journey, he read some stories in *The Daily Telegraph* and flicked through some social media posts on an iPad that was built into the car's back seat console. He always took the back seat – left hand side – and never bothered with the seat belt. He didn't drive himself any more. It wasted too much time and, anyway, there were some legal issues…

Ambrose was a good-looking and well-built fifty-three, with a good head of hair for his age. He smiled briefly as he thought of the lunch he had planned today with Rebecca, a journalist, who was a stunner and seemed to be quite taken with him. This would be their second lunch in a week. Ambrose had no illusions about the ladies though. He was quite prepared to love them and leave them, believing himself an expert not only in getting attractive women into bed but also in finding a way to extract himself from the emotional turmoil afterwards. He sometimes thought slightly fondly of his conquests, but he had convinced himself early on in his somewhat predatory career that most of his ladies had got what they sought – promotion, opportunity, glamorous adventures – and so had he. He always picked the ambitious types – they were more likely to tire of his demands and move on to a bigger fool.

After lunch – at the Savoy Grill no less – he felt a bit the worse for wear and couldn't understand why. He had shared two bottles of a rather nice Wolf Blass Shiraz with Rebecca, who had not disappointed him. She had matched him glass for glass and finally agreed to meet at the weekend at a riverside pub in Henley, once frequented by Charles I. He would book a room and had plenty of persuasive lines that would get her into it – not that it seemed likely to be difficult. He felt supremely confident that he just had to be himself – witty, charming, and clearly both influential and rich. It rarely failed. The less pleasant character traits he was good at keeping under wraps, other than with Doris.

He staggered slightly down the flight of stairs into the Savoy's elegant lobby, bidding Rebecca farewell with a bit more than a peck on the cheek. She looked back at him and smiled when she reached the door and he suddenly felt quite dizzy. That had been happening quite a lot over the past few days – he wondered what it was.

(3)

Sipping a daiquiri and watching the sunset, Selby continued to be troubled but not depressed. He was still close to his wife although they had decided they could not live together at the stage they had reached. He regretted not being able to contact her, or anyone else. But there it is – the loneliness of the long-distance executioner.

Nevertheless, the unmistakable feeling of having achieved something that could transform the grim state of his country was drifting over him. It was almost a recovery of the joy he had once had in life but lost. His thoughts turned to deep background. That conversation at Oxford all those years ago that had been so formative in more ways than one. It was Simmonds – Alasdair, or was it Anthony Simmonds? Yes, of course, Anthony – he insisted on calling himself Anthony with a 'th'.

"I simply don't believe it's a solution at all. It doesn't make sense. It's not rational – cuts across all democratic principles. Extrajudicial killing simply can't be a tool of policy in a civilised world." Simmonds was arguing heatedly as he and Selby crossed the quad.

Selby was quiet for a few moments but responded thoughtfully.

"I'd like to believe it's irrational, but I'm not sure I do any more. What are the alternatives? Let's face it, this is not a civilised world."

"You're taking Jenner too seriously, John." Simmonds was getting really agitated. "I'd have someone drummed out of the University for saying things like that, whether Jenner's a don or not."

"So much for academic freedom then!" returned Selby.

"Too much freedom is no freedom at all," the younger man snapped back. Selby thought that sounded more like taxi-driver wisdom than that of a philosophy research student, but decided not to say so. Instead, Selby chuckled, attempting to defuse the conversation, while Simmonds started to wave his arms about and draw attention to himself.

"Oh, don't get so worked up, Anthony. We don't have any good answers," Selby began. "I don't know what the solution is. But anyway, Jenner's in no position to do anything about it. It's all thousands of miles away – it was just a rant."

"A mighty malevolent one, though," Simmonds replied, more quietly.

They had reached the porters' lodge by now and Selby was about to enter his staircase, a cup of tea and an hour's read of *The Guardian* in mind.

"Don't worry about it, Anthony. Jenner's just a common-room acquaintance. Arguments like that blow over. Just winding you up, I reckon."

Simmonds regained something of his customary cool. "Maybe. It's just scary that's all. If it was a wind-up, it worked like a charm. Made me look a fool."

Simmonds clambered onto his bike and set off back to his digs. Selby made his way up to his rooms and sat down with the paper in front of the empty fireplace. He realised that he had been struck by what Jenner had said. He felt sorry for Simmonds, who had made a scene and had not received the support he was expecting from Selby and the others on the fringe of the conversation.

Jenner had been pontificating, in the usual subdued style, about the rise of Ahmed Abdurrahman Zafaar to the presidency of a small Asian state. Zafaar, claimed Jenner, was a particularly dangerous man because he was attempting to play off both sides of the renewed Cold War against each other. He invited the Americans in to advise on high technology projects, such as power grids and secure government data centres, but at the same time was wooing the Russians with promises of buying huge quantities of military equipment for no obvious purpose. He seemed, explained Jenner, to welcome the sharp diplomatic exchanges that were occurring almost weekly between the two fading superpowers, each megalomaniac leader accusing the other of interfering in the country's internal affairs. The Chinese seemed to be looking on with amusement, playing their cards carefully.

Meanwhile, Zafaar encouraged the Americans to talk about protecting their investments by military means. He gave the Russians a platform to complain about Western economic imperialism. What he hoped to gain was unclear, but it was more than likely to do with a shortage of money. Jenner reckoned that the man was running his country into the ground while acquiring what funds there were for his own benefit. Increasing international tension was just a distraction – collateral damage from his personal greed – about which Zafaar cared nothing.

Simmonds had passionately advocated an approach by the UN, insisting that it must be possible to make Zafaar see sense by rational discussion, showing him the true facts of the situation. All the response he got was a round of laughter from the small group listening in and someone yelling, "There speaks the dog returning to its own vomit – hail the Philosopher."

Jenner eyed the deflated Simmonds like a piece of gristle someone had just spat out and the other three parties to the conversation, including Selby, began to look distinctly uncomfortable. Both the disputants were taking this discussion far too personally.

"Anthony, you're just being hopelessly naïve about this," Jenner crooned patronisingly. The expression was almost one of pity. "The man will not listen to reason. He is not rational. He is a clever bigot with absolute power and a large Swiss bank account." The voice was quiet but grimly determined.

"Nonsense," expostulated Simmonds. "Anyone can see the position he's in. It must be possible to make him see it. Besides, if powerful people like him won't listen to reason, what the hell can you do?"

Silence. Jenner had been preparing for this.

"You kill them," she said.

*